## Train Keeps a'Rollin

Karl crouched, reaching for both his revolver and his knife. Longarm kicked him so hard in the crotch that the impact shot up into his own knee. The big half-breed lurched forward, bounding off his heels toward Longarm, his eyes on fire. The lawman took one step to his left, grabbed the half-breed's collar with one hand, and heaved him out of the vestibule into open air.

There was a thud audible even above the roar of the iron wheels and the shriek of the wind as the big body was smacked hard by the second coach car. Karl screamed shrilly as he fell straight down on the tracks.

The scream died abruptly.

# DON'T MISS THESE
## ALL-ACTION WESTERN SERIES
### FROM THE BERKLEY PUBLISHING GROUP

**THE GUNSMITH by J. R. Roberts**

Clint Adams was a legend among lawmen, outlaws, and ladies. They called him . . . the Gunsmith.

**LONGARM by Tabor Evans**

The popular long-running series about Deputy U.S. Marshal Custis Long—his life, his loves, his fight for justice.

**SLOCUM by Jake Logan**

Today's longest-running action Western. John Slocum rides a deadly trail of hot blood and cold steel.

**BUSHWHACKERS by B. J. Lanagan**

An action-packed series by the creators of Longarm! The rousing adventures of the most brutal gang of cutthroats ever assembled—Quantrill's Raiders.

**DIAMONDBACK by Guy Brewer**

Dex Yancey is Diamondback, a Southern gentleman turned con man when his brother cheats him out of the family fortune. Ladies love him. Gamblers hate him. But nobody pulls one over on Dex . . .

**WILDGUN by Jack Hanson**

The blazing adventures of mountain man Will Barlow—from the creators of Longarm!

**TEXAS TRACKER by Tom Calhoun**

J.T. Law: the most relentless—and dangerous—manhunter in all Texas. Where sheriffs and posses fail, he's the best man to bring in the most vicious outlaws—for a price.

## TABOR EVANS

# LONGARM

### AND THE PLEASANT VALLEY WAR

**J**

JOVE BOOKS, NEW YORK

**THE BERKLEY PUBLISHING GROUP**
**Published by the Penguin Group**
**Penguin Group (USA) Inc.**
**375 Hudson Street, New York, New York 10014, USA**
Penguin Group (Canada), 90 Eglinton Avenue East, Suite 700, Toronto, Ontario M4P 2Y3, Canada
(a division of Pearson Penguin Canada Inc.)
Penguin Books Ltd., 80 Strand, London WC2R 0RL, England
Penguin Group Ireland, 25 St. Stephen's Green, Dublin 2, Ireland (a division of Penguin Books Ltd.)
Penguin Group (Australia), 250 Camberwell Road, Camberwell, Victoria 3124, Australia
(a division of Pearson Australia Group Pty. Ltd.)
Penguin Books India Pvt. Ltd., 11 Community Centre, Panchsheel Park, New Delhi—110 017, India
Penguin Group (NZ), 67 Apollo Drive, Rosedale, North Shore 0632, New Zealand
(a division of Pearson New Zealand Ltd.)
Penguin Books (South Africa) (Pty.) Ltd., 24 Sturdee Avenue, Rosebank, Johannesburg 2196,
South Africa

Penguin Books Ltd., Registered Offices: 80 Strand, London WC2R 0RL, England

This is a work of fiction. Names, characters, places, and incidents either are the product of the author's imagination or are used fictitiously, and any resemblance to actual persons, living or dead, business establishments, events, or locales is entirely coincidental.

LONGARM AND THE PLEASANT VALLEY WAR

A Jove Book / published by arrangement with the author

PRINTING HISTORY
Jove edition / November 2009

Copyright © 2009 by Penguin Group (USA) Inc.
Cover illustration by Miro Sinovcic.

ISBN: 978-0-515-14731-5

JOVE®
Jove Books are published by The Berkley Publishing Group,
a division of Penguin Group (USA) Inc.,
375 Hudson Street, New York, New York 10014.
JOVE® is a registered trademark of Penguin Group (USA) Inc.
The "J" design is a trademark of Penguin Group (USA) Inc.

PRINTED IN THE UNITED STATES OF AMERICA
10  9  8  7  6  5  4  3  2  1

# Chapter 1

The silent night was shattered by the crack of a branch under the boot of a stealthy stalker.

Deputy U.S. Marshal Custis Long, his senses honed by years of man-tracking and its accompanying perils, snapped his eyes open and lifted his head from his saddle. Instantly, he clawed his Frontier Model Colt .44 from the holster wrapped in its cartridge belt beside him and thumbed the hammer back.

Deputy Long—known as Longarm to friend and foe far and wide—extended the cocked pistol in the direction from which the crack had sounded, stretching his lips back from his teeth as he snarled, "One more step, you bushwhackin' son of a bitch, and I'll give you a third eye you won't—!"

*"Custis!"*

Longarm blinked, and slackened his trigger finger.

No slit-eyed, unshaven would-be bushwhacker stood before him, crouched over his campfire with a cocked shooting iron aimed at the lawman's liver. In fact, there was no campfire. The tall, rangy lawman wasn't even outside. He was in a sprawling, well-appointed boudoir, the air perfumed with the faint musk of cherries, and with a wagon-sized, canopied bed upon which his long, naked frame was drawn as taut as that of a docked ship's mooring rope.

A girl wearing only a sheer silk wrapper quaked before him, leaning back against a scrolled oak dresser, her wrapper hanging open to reveal the deep cleavage between her full, firm, pear-shaped, porcelain-pale breasts. One delicate foot rested atop the other, a naked thigh drawn protectively inward and faintly quivering.

"Ah, shit," Longarm grumbled, his ears instantly warming with chagrin. He lifted the Colt's barrel and depressed the hammer. "Sorry, Cynthia. I heard a snap, and I thought . . ."

The sexily regal Cynthia Larimer removed her hands from the edge of the dresser behind her and unexpectedly chuckled, her full, rich lips spreading and her cobalt-blue eyes sparkling in the wan dawn light pushing through the curtains.

"You heard the fire pop, you fool," she said as Longarm returned his Colt to the holster hanging from the bedpost beside him. "I just added some piñon to make the room smell nice, and one of the branches must have had some sap in it."

"Damn—sounded just like a branch snappin' under some yellow-toothed death-dealer's boot!"

Longarm chewed his thick, brown mustache as he looked around the room, still trying to drive out the uncannily real feeling of being out in the tall and uncut, and having an interloper drawing a bead on his chest. He gave a little start as the large fieldstone hearth popped once more, and then he glanced at Cynthia.

"Sure am sorry, girl. Hope I didn't scare you too bad. Don't know what gets into me sometimes. Too long on the owlhoot trail, I reckon."

"Holy mackerel," Cynthia purred, a strange, slack look crossing her finely sculpted, slightly flushed cheeks. "You sure are fast with that thing."

"Had some practice, I reckon." Longarm lay back on the bed and ran his hands through his thick, brown hair. "What're you doin' up, anyways? Didn't know you to rise till nearly noon." He chuckled.

"I remembered that you said you had to leave early, so last night, when we'd snuck in after the policeman's ball, I told the kitchen girls I'd like a breakfast tray brought up to my room around six-thirty. I was just now checking the time."

Cynthia's voice was so thick that Longarm lifted his head to regard her curiously. Her sparking eyes were sliding across his broad, naked chest and down his long, naked legs.

"What's the matter?" he said. "I didn't give ya a heart seizure, did I?" The strain in his thighs and lower back reminded him of their rather strenuous sexual athletics of a few hours ago. "A girl in as good a shape as you . . . ?"

He drew the several quilts and blankets up over himself, as it was late fall in Denver, the growing cow town sprawled beneath the Rockies' Front Range, and the nights and mornings were chill.

"You certainly did."

Cynthia's chest was heaving, her breasts rising and falling sharply behind her see-through wrapper. The light was murky, but Longarm thought her nipples were stiffening.

"Custis, something happened to me when I saw you aiming that big gun at me," she said breathily. "Not sure what it was exactly. Maybe it was how a killing fire came into those savagely narrowed eyes of yours. Maybe it was how the muscles in your arms leaped and coiled like snakes just beneath the skin, the big muscles in your chest standing out like stone slabs." She lowered her chin and swallowed hard. "But my heart is drumming, and my knees are feeling so *weeeak!*"

The girl's breasts were swollen. Her face was mottled red. Her lust was catching. Longarm felt his own body temperature rising. He patted the bed beside him and frowned with mock concern.

"Maybe you better crawl back into bed, then, sugar. Take a load off. Let ol' Custis . . . uh . . . massage your back and other sundry parts."

Cynthia placed her hand on her chest. "I forget sometimes, Custis, with all our silly playing around, that you're one of the greatest lawmen in all the West. That you have put fear and trembling in the hearts of many a badman . . . and likely have turned a good number toe-down, as they say in the yellow-backed novels."

"Ah, hell," Longarm said with a self-effacing chuff, feeling his member stiffen down beneath the covers as he stared at the girl's pebbling nipples and the tuft of silky black hair between her thighs. "I reckon someone's gotta protect the innocent, punish the lawbreakers." He swallowed. "Like I said, you best come back to bed, Miss Cynthia, and let me administer some tender care to your obvious . . . uh . . . *strained nerves.*"

The leggy, raven-haired Larimer heiress started toward the bed. She wore only the sheer wrap, the tails of which fluttered about thighs that were slender but tight from riding her uncle's finely blooded Thoroughbreds and Tennessee trotters all about their impeccably landscaped Sherman Hill estate.

When she wasn't on one of her frequent world tours, that was.

In her mere twenty-two years, Cynthia Larimer had visited more countries than Longarm knew the names of. She and he had met about a year ago. They'd been introduced to each other by Cynthia's uncle, General Larimer—that is, William Larimer III, considered by most to be Denver's founding father, after whom a good many streams, streets, counties, and babies had been named.

Longarm and Cynthia hadn't fallen so much in love as in lust, neither being at all ready for the traditional banal commitments, even if such commitments had been possible given the pair's class differences—he, a pistol-packing public servant; she, a world-class heiress who would naturally follow the silver spoon jutting from her bee-stung lips into the palace of some European prince, say, or into the coifed and manicured grounds of a rich East Coast industrialist's estate.

So the improbable pair—the cultured princess and the roguish lawman whose storied past had found its way into many an illustrated newspaper and dime novel—got together to frolic whenever they both found themselves in Denver at the same time. So people wouldn't talk, as people were wont to do, especially about the moneyed Larimers, and so the general and Mrs. Larimer would find nothing untoward about their fraternization, Longarm pretended to be merely the beautiful young heiress's escort and bodyguard, whose intentions were merely protective, as opposed to seductive.

However, being a filly as headstrong as any of those in her uncle's stables, and downright defiant at times, Cynthia found the masquerade silly, and this inattention to appearances on her part had often proven not only embarrassing but dangerous.

It had all come to a head, as it were, when, during a party at the Larimer estate last Christmas, they'd both tread to within a few seconds of discovery by the general himself in the general's second-floor libary/office—Cynthia on her hands and knees beneath the general's desk with Longarm's fully engorged cock in her mouth.

Now she sat on the edge of the bed and leaned over the tall, rugged lawman, running her hands through the hair on his broad chest and grinding her fingers into shoulders that were as solid as wheel hubs. Her breathing was labored.

"Custis," she said. "Oh, Custis, you are quite a man!"

He rose to a half-sitting position and placed his hands over her breasts through the gauzy silk of the wrapper. As they moved together, massaging and caressing, the bedsprings began to squeak faintly.

"Easy," he whispered. "You said the general and your aunt are on the premises, correct?"

"Don't worry about them."

"I'd like to not have to worry about 'em, but it's me who'll be flyin' out the window if the general comes callin' with that big Russian-made bird gun of his."

Cynthia slid a hand down beneath the covers and wrapped her small, fine-boned hand around his iron-hard cock, and squeezed. She leaned forward, closing her eyes, the flush of sensual pleasure climbing higher in her cheeks.

Longarm closed his own eyes for a moment and groaned as she continued squeezing his staff, sending hot spasms of pleasure throughout his loins. When he opened his eyes again, he saw that she was sprawled beside him with one foot up on the edge of the bed, toes flexed, and her thighs slightly spread. Tender pink flesh shone within the silky darkness of her snatch.

He slipped a finger inside. He didn't have to do much work to get it in. She was warm and moist.

Keeping her eyes closed, she lifted her chin suddenly,

gasped, and squeezed his cock even harder.

Longarm's heart leaped slightly, and he stuck his finger farther into the girl's warm, wet center, and sort of turned it while at the same time massaging the delicate, petal-like folds of flesh at its opening. She squirmed around, sighing and groaning, running her fist slowly up and down Longarm's cock, which was now so hard he thought the skin would split and the big, mushroom head pop open.

When Longarm had the girl sopping wet and shuddering, he stuck another thick, brown finger into her core. She gave a start, rising up on the heel of her foot slightly and stopping the manipulation of Longarm's organ briefly, as though in sudden shock. She half-croaked, half-muttered something and stretched her lips back from her perfect white teeth.

Then, laughing crazily, she began pumping him harder. He groaned and grunted, arching his back, as she moaned and shifted her taut, round bottom around on the bed beside him, her full breasts jerking and sliding on her chest.

Suddenly, she dropped her head over his cock and dribbled a dollop of spit onto its blossoming purple head.

She let the saliva roll down the sides of his cock, and then she began pumping him again, but faster now, working him into a veritable lather as he continued fingering the girl's steaming pussy.

"Oh, Custis!" she groaned. "Oh . . . good Lord, help me . . . *Custis!*"

He sighed, cursed, shook his head, threw it back on his shoulders, and squeezed his eyes closed. He stretched his left leg straight out on the bed, keeping the right curled beneath his other knee, and hardened his jaws as his fingers danced around between Cynthia's legs, her own juices now bathing his knuckles that were now nearly all the way inside her. He felt his blood rising to a fast boil, and he gritted his teeth, wanting to savor every second of the incredibly erotic swelling inside him as the girl pumped him faster and faster with both hands.

She leaned over his chest while keeping her thighs spread, trying hard to muffle her grunts and excited laughs as they both rose to the height of their mutual passions.

"*Christ,*" Longarm muttered, barely parting his lips.

He'd had handjobs before, but nothing to equal this. Somehow he felt more closely united with the delectable girl than if he'd been hammering away between her legs. It was as though they were both sound asleep, spirits entwined, and enjoying the same improbably wonderful wet dream.

Longarm delayed his climax as long as he could, tearing at the sheets with his free hand. Then Cynthia let out a yelp as his fountain erupted, spurting his creamy jism across his belly and chest, a couple of rounds landing just short of his neck, one or two splattering the underside of Cynthia's chin.

She continued to pump as she, too, came, throwing her head back on her shoulders and laughing at the ceiling as though she'd completely lost her marbles. Longarm's seed ran in two slender rivulets down her neck and into the valley between her breasts.

When she was finished shuddering and jerking, lifting her rump from the sheets, she splayed her hand across his dwindling cock and his balls, and mashed her breasts against his jism-slick chest.

Her shoulders jerked once more, and then she lay still. He could feel her breasts mashing against him as she breathed.

Longarm sighed, ran his hands through the girl's hair. "*Whew!*"

Cynthia lightly caressed his balls with her fingers.

A knock sounded on the door.

She jerked her head up. Her mouth opened wide as she stared in shock at Longarm. He returned the look, his brown eyes incredulous.

Cynthia cleared her throat and in her calmest voice possible said, "Yes? Who is it, please?"

A girl cleared her throat, then said in a slightly puzzled, skeptical tone, "Your breakfast, Miss Larimer."

# Chapter 2

Longarm cast a cautious glance around him as he jogged between the Larimer stables and headed for Sherman Avenue beyond.

No one was on the Larimer grounds except two stable boys, cursing each other as they tried to reset a corral gate, and a few robins digging for rooms in the barnyard. The old general himself was likely in his office, furtively stirring sherry into his morning coffee while perusing the *Rocky Mountain News*.

When Longarm had slipped through the poplars lining the cinder-paved avenue, nodding to the driver of a passing coal wagon, he was thoroughly winded. Climbing down the rickety trellis from Cynthia's window after the heavy breakfast she'd ordered for him—three eggs, a boatload of bacon, and a towering stack of sourdough pancakes—had been no easy task. And there was always the chance the general was waiting for him on the grounds below with that big popper some Russian royal had given him on one of his world tours, and which had been written about in all the big-city news rags.

Longarm stopped by one of the gas lamps the all-too-civilized city had recently installed, and, catching his breath and watching a shaggy collie dog lift its leg on a lamppost across the street, he dug in a breast pocket of his shirt for a three-for-a-nickel cheroot and a lucifer. A vagrant morning breeze with a chill fall nip touched the brim of his flat-topped brown Stetson, ruffled his John L. Sullivan mustache, and twisted his string tie up around his neck.

His normal attire was a three-piece business suit of tobacco tweed, a little wild and woolly around the edges, with skintight whipcord trousers, and .44 Frontier Colt holstered in a cross-draw rig high on his left hip. That's what he wore this frosty Monday morning. It was a morning that saw him—a little too early after his carnal high jinks all weekend with Cynthia Larimer (Had they really done it in a pumpkin patch on the poor side of Cherry Creek, or had he been hit on the head by badmen a few too many times?)—headed to the Federal Building to palaver awhile with his boss, Chief Marshal Billy Vail. After the meeting, he'd likely be heading off to sundry parts of the West on another assignment, and he wouldn't see Cynthia again for another couple of months.

He chuckled again dryly as he snapped the lucifer to life on his shell belt and, firing the long, black cheroot, watched the collie dog shuffle off to desecrate another gas lamp. Longarm and Cynthia were going to get caught. He had a bad feeling. After running more than his share of badmen to ground and either turning them toe-down or sending them off for a lifelong sojourn in the federal lockup, he'd likely go out bloody in bed.

Riddled with ten-gauge buck.

But, damn. The tall, rangy, sun-seasoned lawman shook his head, remembering how Cynthia's hands had expertly plied him, and the feel of her snatch wrapped like a furry wet glove around his hand. What a way to go!

Taking back streets and enjoying the warm sun penetrating the knife-like air rolling down from the snow-mantled crest of Long's Peak in the west, he made his way to Capitol Hill. He pinched his hat brim at a couple of rather drab female secretaries who regarded him coyly from beneath their feathered picture hats, and took the broad marble steps two at a time as he headed inside the Federal Building.

On the second floor he found the old familiar door marked "UNITED STATES MARSHAL, FIRST DISTRICT COURT OF COLORADO", which he shouldered open before tossing his hat onto the hat tree just inside.

"Mornin', Henry," he called. "How the hell's it hangin' this bright, crisp, Monday mornin'?"

Playing his typewriter with his back to his desk and to Longarm, the prissy secretary merely sniffed and, without so much as slowing the practiced movements of his long, fine-boned fingers, said, "Marshal Vail will you see, Deputy Long."

"Henry," Longarm said, planting his fists at the edge of the secretary's small but immaculate desk and leaning forward, "after all these years, don't you think you could call me Custis?"

Henry lifted his fingers from the typewriter keys and sighed with practiced impatience. To the officious-looking books lined across the wall in front of him, he said, "I take it you had a lovely weekend of rampant self-indulgence and generally all-around indecent activities, Deputy Long. Congratulations. Say hello to the Devil for me. As for the moment, Marshal Vail will see you."

His fingers dropped to the keys once more, and the tooth-gnashing clatter resumed.

"Henry, damnit, you're wasting your youth," Longarm said. "Why don't you let me take you out some Friday night and introduce you around? I know some purty little gals that could take the starch outta that stiff collar of yourn, not to mention your shorts."

"Oh, I'm quite positive you do," Henry said above the clatter. "And thanks for the invitation, Deputy. It just so happens, however, that I'll be busy for the next several years!"

Longarm shook his head as he strode around the end of the secretary's desk. "Well, damnit, I reckon I tried." He headed for the door, across the frosted glass upper panel of which was marked in no-frills gold-leaf lettering: "CHIEF MARSHAL WILLIAM VAIL." He knocked twice and went in.

"Amazing how that little feller can play the typewriter and talk at the same time. I don't see how he does it, Chief. You ever tried to play one of those things? I don't see how you could think of anything else, especially playin' them keys as fast as Henry does!"

Chief Marshal Billy Vail lifted his balding head from the paperwork and bookwork spread before him on his wagon-sized desk, removing a cigar from his mouth and blowing out a heavy cloud of aromatic blue smoke. "Leave the kid alone," he growled as Longarm angled the red Moroccan leather guest chair in front of the stout oak desk. "His mother was on the scrap this weekend, and he had to do all the cooking and cleaning. Even had to feed her chickens and them feisty geese. Henry's ma and my wife must share the same broomstick." The chief marshal scowled through his round spectacles as he slammed closed the ledger he'd been scribbling in. "I swear the woman's part nun, like one o' them half-crazed, wild-eyed sisters I see every Sunday in church. How I ever got myself . . ."

Vail shook his head and leaned back in his chair. "Never mind. Just take my advice, Custis, and never get married."

"Don't intend to, Chief. Sorry about the doin's at home. Or . . . uh . . . lack thereof."

"Like I said," the chief marshal said, shaking his head again and taking several small puffs from the fat stogie, "never get married, less'n you never wanna get it again."

Suddenly, the pudgy chief lawdog convulsed and, coughing loudly, waved the heavy smoke cloud from in front of his face with a stout arm, his rolled white shirt-sleeve revealing a stretch of fish-belly skin spotted with freckles and tufted with fine, sandy hair. "Jesus Christ, here I am discussing my sex life with the most oversexed son of a bitch in Denver. What the hell's got into me?"

He grabbed a manila folder off the stack beside him and gave it a toss. It landed on Longarm's lap with a thump—three inches of immaculate pages typed by none other than the prissy, home-bound, apron-tied secretary himself, whose incessant clatter Longarm could feel through the floor beneath his boots.

Longarm riffled through the carbon copy pages. "What's this?"

"Trouble down Texas way. Place called Pleasant Valley, of all the ludicrous names."

"What's the trouble, chief?"

"You name it—rustling, land fight, murder. This one's pretty much got it all." Billy Vail drew deep on the cigar as he lounged back in his leather swivel chair and thumbed his glasses up his nose. "'Pears there's a ranch down thataway. One of those big fuckin' Texas-sized affairs. Half a million acres spread across four counties and owned by a British investment company and ramrodded by a Scot named Horace Woolyard. The company bought and expanded the

Pleasant Valley Ranch after a dozen or so other outfits had leased state school land in the same area. Woolyard fenced in the whole fuckin' affair, including those ranchers that were already there."

"Doesn't sound too neighborly," Longarm said, pursing his lips as he flipped through the packet on his lap. "But common enough nowadays since old Glidden invented bobwire." He closed the folder and dug in his shirt pocket for a cigar. "So the boys that got themselves fenced in to a bigger ranch have a bone to pick with the setup? Maybe doin' a little rustlin', a little killin'? Or is this bigger Pleasant Valley outfit tryin' to drive them out with a little killin', long-ropin', and maybe even some lynchin' an' such? Either way, sounds a whole lot like a whole lotta little misunderstandings spread here and there about the entire frontier."

"Sounds like it because it is. The problem here is there was no problem for nigh on three years, after the Pleasant Valley boys fenced themselves—and the smaller ranchers—in. But then the number crunchers over England way decided to do a little bean counting and discovered that the third largest outfit in all of Texas wasn't making any money. Not a dime. In fact, they were losing thousands of dollars every year."

"Rustling," Longarm said with a grunt, firing his long, black cheroot and tossing the match into an ashtray on his boss's desk.

"Sure." Vail waved his hand in front of his face, making a sour expression. "Jesus Christ, you smoke the most foul-smelling tobacco known to man. You know, if you invested in some of those cheap, black Mexican cheroots that'd gag a dog off a gut wagon, you'd be making an improvement, Custis!"

"If I could afford those fifty-centers, Billy, I'd smoke

'em. But since I'm the only one more poorly paid than the
street sweepers in spite of my risking life and limb every
time I step outside, I'll have to stick with these three-fer-a-
nickels." Longarm looked at the smoking coal at the end of
the long, slender cigar. "Matter of fact, they've sorta
growed on me over the years."

"Lord love a duck," Vail said, swatting at the smoke
once more. "Anyways . . . your train's headed for Claireville, Texas. Shouldn't take you more than three days'
travel. I hear these new cow catchers they have nowadays
are so sturdy the engineers don't have to slow down a bit
unless there's a whole herd on the tracks."

"Claireville, huh?"

"Heard of it?"

"Been through there a few times. Wasn't much but
prickly pear and tumbleweeds last time I was there. A
church and three saloons as I recall. One wasn't half-bad."

"I'm sure you'll investigate its current condition."

"So, tell me, Billy—ain't this a job normally under the
jurisdiction of the Texas Rangers?"

"It is at that. Problem is, three Texas Rangers were
found nestling with rattlesnakes on Pleasant Valley range.
All laid out beneath the big live oak from which, judging
by the nooses still dangling from a stout limb and by the
lengths the Rangers' necks had been stretched, they'd been
hanged."

"Ah."

"We've been called in by the commander of a Ranger
station over by Cactus Gulch. He doesn't trust his men to
be able to investigate the murders in an unbiased manner.
Adding to the complication here is the fact that almost
every Texan living in these four counties is part of a feuding
bunch of folks from somewhere in the middle of Texas. As

you know, there was practically another civil war down there after the Big Misunderstanding Between the States, when the carpetbaggers moved in with their own brand of law, piss-burning the old-salt Texans real good!"

"Yeah, I remember. And there's no deadlier bunch of diamondbacks in any nest anywhere north of the Rio Grande." Longarm puffed smoke and tapped the edge of the file folder against his palm. "Well, when's my train leave? Henry have my train tickets, expense vouchers?"

"Hold on a second, you wild lobo." Vail scowled at his deputy through the smoke billowing in storm-sized clouds above his desk. "Don't you wanna know who your contacts are?"

"Oh, I reckon I should."

Vail gave a wry chuff. "You're to meet a stock detective named Hank Tremaine and a sergeant of the Rangers, Ebenezer Hall, at the sheriff's office in Claireville—time to be determined after you get there and report in with the sheriff. Tremaine's out of Fort Worth, but he works for the Pleasant Valley outfit. He's an ex-Buffalo soldier. I forget the Claireville County sheriff's name, but he's a one-legged gent probably given the badge out of pity and for his service for the Confederacy during the War of Yankee Aggression. That's how things work down there, don't ya know."

"So, this Hall's a Ranger?" Longarm asked, arching a brow.

Vail nodded. "About the only one the Ranger commander trusts not to go lynching the first hombre he remembers from the old feuds a few miles to the east. Besides, I've sent orders for him and Hall to sit tight till you get there. And the ramrod at the Pleasant Valley Ranch has agreed to stop swapping lead with the other ranchers till you get a handle on the situation, too."

"There been a lotta lead-swappin' of late down thataway, Billy?"

"For the past year and a half, that range has turned bright red. Besides them Rangers, ranchers, stock detectives, cowboys from the Pleasant Valley outfit . . . a good nine, ten men and even a settler's wife been turned under. And it's gonna get worse if you can't grab the tiger by the tail, and grab it quick."

Longarm nodded and tapped the folder in his hand again. "All right, then, Billy, if that's all. Henry has the train tickets?" He heaved himself out of his chair.

His boss scowled across the desk at him, incredulous. "What, no complaints? No accusations that here I go sending your poor lone hide off to the wolves one more time, and that I best start looking for a new man to take your place on account of all the lead you're likely to run into on a mission that rightly requires the services of the *whole U.S. Army*?"

Longarm hiked a shoulder. "Well, shit, Billy, I reckon I'm used to it."

Vail stared at him, a smile slowly lifting the corners of his mouth, his watery blue eyes sparking knowingly behind his glasses. "Oh, shit."

"What?"

"That little Miss Larimer, the general's prized filly, was in town this past weekend. I read about her in the paper. That's why you're only half here. I thought your eyes looked glazed, but I thought it was maybe those awful cigars of yours, or maybe a bad breakfast, or maybe your landlady finally got tired of your wicked ways and tossed you out on your ear.

"But shit, no—you were fucking the prized niece of Denver's founding father seven ways from sundown! You're so devil-may-care giddy from that ungodly coupling that I could send you down to Arizona to take on the entire bronco Apache nation wearing nothing but your hat and boots and armed with only that little double-barreled popper in your vest pocket, and you'd just nod and give me that shit-eating look and say, 'When do I catch the train, Billy!'"

"Billy, I done told you—Cynthia and I are friends. The general has asked me to accompany her to her sundry society events such as the theater and the policeman's ball and so on to make sure she is unharassed by the soiled denizens of Denver's back streets and stables."

Billy Vail leaped to his feet, his pudgy face flushed with exasperation as he poked his stogie at Longarm. "Don't give me that ole saw, Custis, goddamnit! If I've told you once, I've told you a thousand times to cease and desist from the diddling of that little miss fancy-schmantsy, or you're gonna end up in a bad, bad way. For God's sake, man, don't you realize what kind of political pull the general *has* around here? If he finds out his prized niece—the one we always see his arm wrapped around on page two of the *Rocky Mountains News*—spends the brunt of her weekends here on her back, with the likes of your lowly, law-dawging, pistol-packing self riding her hard and putting her up wet, he'll have to merely snap his fingers and blink an eye, and I'll likely get the word handed down from on high to give you the pointed-toed boot into early retirement!"

Longarm laughed despite knowing that his boss was right, despite knowing that he could no more stop frolicking with the raven-haired, heavy-breasted, salty but refined Miss Cynthia Larimer than give up his Maryland rye or his cigars, or, for that matter, breathing! "Well, then, I reckon you'll have to find somebody else to kick around, Billy!"

"Get outta here, you big, stubborn pile of horseshit! Your train leaves at three, so go home and scour those visions of doin' that girl doggie style out of your pea-pickin' brain! You're gonna need to be clearheaded down there in Pleasant Valley!"

"See you when I get back, Billy!" Longarm called as he quickly drew the door closed behind him.

In the outer office, Henry had stopped playing his typewriter, and now Longarm saw the prissy secretary sitting statue-still in his chair, hands frozen above the keys, one ear cocked toward the wall. With a startled, wide-eyed glance at the big lawman who was starting for the hat tree, Henry lowered his hands to the typewriter once more.

"Your tickets are on my desk there, Deputy," he sang above the near-deafening clatter.

"Thanks, Henry," Longarm said as, setting his hat on his head, he moved to the desk. "If you spread around anything you just heard in there, amigo, when I come back from Texas I'll whup you eight ways from February."

Henry stopped the typewriter's clatter long enough to say, "I read the report. You may not come back this time." He sniffed. "Pity."

The clatter resumed a wink after what Longarm thought was a squawk of laughter.

"I always come back," he grumbled, stuffing the railroad tickets in his coat pocket and heading out.

# Chapter 3

Longarm did as his boss Billy Vail had ordered—at least as far as heading home to his rented digs on the poor side of Cherry Creek and catching forty winks, anyway. It wasn't so easy, however, to scour the remembered images and sensations of his week—the most athletic and adventurous one so far, to be sure—with the delectable Cynthia Larimer. But when he woke just after noon, he felt noticeably more refreshed than he had when he'd awakened the first time that day, just before the best handjob he'd ever experienced.

Holy-moly, that girl had pure Chinese silk for hands, and the engine of a damn Baldwin locomotive for a sexual appetite!

Packing his usual traveling gear—McClellan saddle, Winchester rifle, war bag filled with possibles, including underwear, handcuffs, spare .44 shells, and a fresh bottle of Tom Moore Maryland rye—Longarm left his rented rooms and headed down to Larimer Street for chili and beer in one of his favorite hole-in-the wall eateries. When he'd finished the meal, he sipped another beer and smoked a cheroot while reading half of the day's paper. Around two-thirty, he loaded all his gear onto one shoulder, hefted his rifle in his right hand, and started the tramp down the hill toward Union Station.

He had the station's big arched doors in sight when suddenly, out of the blue, the hair beneath his starched collar pricked, and a couple of muscles between his anvil-sized shoulder blades twitched. In the midst of the depot walking traffic, he stopped and looked around, a frown wrinkling one cinnamon brow.

Nothing back there out of the usual. Just your usual grip-carrying, check-suited whiskey drummers and a smattering of trail waddies in long dusters balancing Texas saddles on their shoulders as they made their way to the station, spurs ringing and raking on the sun-seasoned pink cobbles. Beyond was the low sandstone-block wall running between the depot grounds and Wynkoop Street. Nothing in the street but the usual hacks and red-wheeled buggies commandeered by top-hatted drivers in broad-cloth cloaks, with a beer wagon clattering along behind a mane-jostling team of manure-spotted, black-and-white Percherons.

Longarm turned a shoulder to avoid a young lady in red-and-white gingham walking too fast and with her head down, and gave his backtrail another careful gander. Relatively certain he wasn't being shadowed, but mystified by the uneasy feeling that had so suddenly washed over him, like a chill wind over a glacier, he turned and continued on into the station.

He'd been ambushed enough times in his eventful career not to dismiss the feeling as a case of raw nerves, however. One, he'd never been given to "nerves," in spite of the danger he'd confronted at nearly every turn in his professional travels, and, two, such a premonition raspily whispered directly into his unconscious brain had more than a few times been followed up with blood and thunder.

Since the Atchison, Topeka and Santa Fe flier was ready and waiting out on the platform, the big locomotive panting like a dying dinosaur and shrouded in coal-black ash from its big, diamond-shaped smokestack, Longarm climbed aboard. He moved down the aisle, twisting and turning under his heavy load to avoid the other boarding passengers, and took a seat with his back to the coach car's front wall, facing the rear. He didn't always sit with his back to a bulkhead, as it was just too damn much work to live as though every trip might be his last, but since the hairs on the back of his neck were still prickling persistently, he decided that putting a wall behind him might be prudent.

He stowed his gear in the racks over his head—all except his Winchester. He leaned the long gun against his right thigh, and it may have been the rifle or his aloof demeanor, his nose buried in the newspaper he'd swiped from the eatery, but no one took the wine-red, plush-upholstered seat beside him or the two facing him. Not until several minutes after the train had pulled out of the station, anyway, and was making its slow climb up the pass just south of Denver and north of Colorado Springs.

The door at the far end of the car swung open, and a spade-bearded gent with a round-brimmed hat and a soiled duster stumbled into the car, swaying from side to side with the train's pitch and jolt. He wore two bandoliers crisscrossed on his chest and two walnut-gripped Colts holstered low on his black denim-clad thighs. As the man looked around, scowling under heavy, dark brows, two other gents stumbled into the car behind him.

One was shorter than the first, moon-faced, blue-eyed, and smiling like a moron. The one behind him was a whole head taller—a big half-breed with long, coal-black hair and a red-and-white beaded bandana around his forehead. He wore a leather jacket over a wool vest, and over the vest he, too, wore crisscrossed bandoliers, every loop filled with a .45 cartridge. He held his head straight forward but slid his eyes around cautiously as he followed the other two men down the car's cluttered aisle, all three tripping over luggage and parasols and, in one case, a cage in which two leghorn chickens squawked and clucked.

From the continued prickling of the hairs under his collar, and from the slow, wry smile he felt tugging at his mouth corners, Longarm knew the men were heading for him even before the first man stopped in the aisle beside him.

He slid his oily eyes toward the seats opposite Longarm. "This seat taken?"

Longarm had been watching the trio in the periphery of his vision. Now he looked over the newspaper he held before him. "Does it look like it?"

The first man, whose skin was pale, in stark contrast to the black of his chin whiskers and upswept mustache, glanced at the men behind him, then tossed his head at the two free seats facing Longarm. Longarm didn't bother pulling his long legs in, so the first man had to sidle awkwardly over to the inside seat, giving Longarm sour looks and cursing under his breath.

The second man, continuing to smile idiotically, a glimmer of pure folly in his soft blue eyes, sat down beside the first. The big half-breed was about to drop into the seat to Longarm's right when the idiot second man leaped out of his seat and into the one the half-breed had been about to take.

The idiot squealed in delight.

The half-breed scowled down at him, as though the idiot were a fresh smear of dog shit he'd suddenly discovered on his boot. The idiot chuckled, and then, continuing to scowl at the round-faced man, the half-breed sank his two-hundred-plus pounds into the chair to the left of the first man, who lifted himself up with a grunt to pull his duster flaps onto his lap and to adjust the pistols on his thighs.

Longarm continued to pretend to read the newspaper, keeping the three obvious scalawags—if they hadn't been the cause of his unease, he was a monkey's uncle—in the periphery of his vision. He tightened his grip on the paper when the first man, straight across from him, rose suddenly from his seat, loudly hacking phlegm, lowered the window, and stuck his face out. He spat downwind, then, pulling his face back into the car and raking a grimy sleeve across his mouth, he closed the window with a *bang* that made Longarm's trigger finger itch, and sank back down in his seat.

Longarm glanced over the top of his paper at the man. The man returned the stare with an insolent one of his own, tipping his head back slightly and to one side. A squawk sounded to Longarm's right. He turned his head slightly to see the moron grinning up at him. The moron's light blue eyes danced from Longarm to the other two men, and Longarm switched his own gaze to the half-breed, who was staring at him blankly.

The lawman had just glanced down to see the Smith & Wesson the half-breed wore in the cross-draw position on his right hip, and the big, bone-handled bowie jutting from a deerskin sheath on his left hip, when a ratcheting click sounded. He might not have heard it above the clatter of the train and the low din of conversation emanating from the rest of the car had he not been waiting for it.

He slid his gaze left along the top edge of his paper, to

the man sitting next to the window. The man stared at him, his two dung-brown eyes looking like twin pools of oil against the pasty white of his cheeks. He wore the same dull expression. His black spade beard was wet from where his spit blew back at him.

Longarm lowered the paper six inches to see the Colt .45 aimed at his belly. The brown-eyed man smiled slightly. The moron to Longarm's right wheezed a devilish laugh. The half-breed stared at Longarm now, and a humorous light had entered his cold gaze. Both his scarred, knotted, roast-sized hands rested on his thighs, not far from the bowie and the Smith & Wesson.

The man holding the .45 canted his head to one side and said just loudly enough to be heard above the train, "That him, Willie?"

The moron reached into his shabby denim jacket and pulled out a folded yellow paper. His small, clawlike hands opened it clumsily, and he held it up, angling it toward the man holding the .45. On the yellow parchment had been drawn a chiseled-featured hombre with a thick longhorn mustache and wearing a flat-brimmed hat. A long, thin cigar protruded from the figure's long, penciled lips.

"Sure looks like him to me," said the moron, loosing another squeaky chuckle.

The half-breed grunted and grinned, opening his mouth. Deep inside that black, snaggletoothed cavern, Longarm saw what remained of the man's tongue—nothing but a small, ragged flap flicking around like the tail of a mouse with its head caught in a trap. Longarm's insides recoiled at the sight, and then he glanced at the paper again.

To the right of his likeness—and a damn fine one, he had to admit—"$2000" had been scrawled in large numbers with heavy lead.

He whistled. "Shit—lookee there. Someone must want my balls pretty damn bad."

"You can keep your balls," said the man aiming the .45 at Longarm's belly button. "We just want your head."

The big half-breed grinned again as he wrapped his right hand around the bone handle of his bowie knife. He said something that, because he had no tongue, sounded like a baby's gurgle.

"That's Karl," the man with the gun said, canting his head toward the half-breed. "He's gonna cut your head off. We're gonna bag it up and take it down to New Mexico."

The half-breed grunted eagerly as he leaned forward and stuck a hand down into the well of one of his knee-high boots. Straightening, he produced a burlap bag with a rope looped around its top. He held the bag up and grinned and chortled again like a baby wanting breakfast.

The moron squealed as he set the lawman's Winchester on the floor. "A whore up in Dakota cut poor Karl's tongue out after he passed out from too much tanglefoot. What he's sayin' is, that's the bag we're gonna take your head back with us to New Mexico in!"

The moron stretched his lips back from his teeth, mewling with delight.

"I sorta got that," Longarm said. "What overfilled privy pit did you three ugly, cork-headed bags of bovine afterbirth crawl up out of, anyway?"

"*Afterbirth*?" the moron exclaimed, indignant. "You hear what he called us, Dietrich?"

"Shut up, Willie." Dietrich jerked the gun barrel up. "Let's take a little walk, lawdog. Outside."

Longarm's gut tightened. His jaws hardened, and his eyes narrowed. "I ain't goin' anywhere with you boys."

"That right? Let me put it this way," Dietrich said. "You

don't go with us nice and quiet-like, Karl's gonna ram that big pigsticker of his through the back of his seat."

Karl glanced over his shoulder, at the bonnet-wearing young mother holding a fussy baby in the seat behind him. Grinning, he turned back to Longarm.

"First," Dietrich said, "you'll turn over that six-shooter. Nice and slow, usin' only two fingers."

Longarm hesitated. He glanced at Dietrich's cocked .45. He looked at Karl, whose big right hand was wrapped around the handle of his bowie knife. From the knife he slid his gaze up and across Karl's massive chest to the baby now facing Longarm over its mother's shoulder. The baby wasn't a year old, and his eyes were wide and blue. His red lips were wet. The kid was staring at Longarm, and his rosy wet lips suddenly spread with a gummy smile.

Karl winked.

Longarm slowly lowered his right hand to the cross-draw rig on his left hip. He released the keeper thong and slid the gun up from the holster by two fingers. When Dietrich had grabbed it and set it on the seat, between him and Karl, the bounty hunter said, "Any more?"

"I always figure if one ain't enough, you shouldn't be packin' any."

"Check him, Willie."

Willie squealed softly again and leaned toward Longarm. He patted the lawman's pockets, even felt around behind him. All the while he was sort of mewling like a lamb in fresh green timothy. He pulled Longarm's old Ingersoll railroad watch from his left vest pocket and dropped it on the lawman's lap.

"That's it," he told Dietrich.

"What's on the other end of his watch chain?" Dietrich said.

Willie removed the end of the gold-washed chain from Longarm's right vest pocket, holding it up so that Dietrich could see the small, dangling gold bar. "Nothin'."

"Can I ask who sent ya?" Longarm said. "Might as well tell me, since my head'll be in the bag soon anyways."

Dietrich's eyes almost crossed as he thought about that, the skin above his nose wrinkling. He glanced at Willie, who hiked a shoulder.

"Name Pink Hutchins ring a bell?" Dietrich asked Longarm.

"An owlhoot I killed a few months ago in the Rockies. No-good thief and bushwhacker."

"Well, his daddy, ole Hutch Hutchins from Las Cruces, took exception." Dietrich's dark eyes smiled. "Up," he told Longarm, just loud enough for only Longarm and the other two men to hear. "Any smart moves, and you're dead. And just cause I'm meaner'n a maverick bull with a bad case of the Mescin clap, I'm gonna pop one through that noisy kid. And then his mouse-faced mother."

Longarm dropped his newspaper and climbed to his feet. He slid one more look around at each of the three men who'd come for his head, then turned and followed Willie and Karl into the aisle. Willie stepped back beside Karl, holding his hand on his pistol grip, that big, cork-headed grin making his eyes flash.

As Longarm turned toward the vestibule door, he glanced once more at Karl's big bowie, the handle of which the man's red fist was still wrapped around.

The wide-bladed pigsticker made Longarm's neck itch. He reached for the door handle and stepped out into the screaming wind.

"That's far enough, lawdog." Flanked by the other two, Dietrich stopped just outside the coach car door and yelled above the wind. "Turn around so's I can say I never shot a man in the back!"

Longarm turned. The gold-chased, double-barreled derringer he'd removed from his vest pocket before the three would-be assassins had taken seats across from him flashed in the afternoon light when he opened his hand. Dietrich had just started to raise his .45 toward Longarm's head.

His eyes snapped wide. Knowing that if he paused to give the man a chance to surrender his own weapon he'd be a headless corpse in seconds, Longarm extended the derringer straight out from his right shoulder and fired.

The pop was nearly drowned by the wind and the train's roar. Dietrich lurched back and fired his .45 into the air. Willie was bringing his old Schofield up, screaming. Longarm plugged the moron through his right cheek.

As Willie flew back against the door, eyes rolling up in his head, Longarm palmed the spent, smoking derringer. Before him, the big half-breed crouched, gritting his teeth and reaching for both his revolver and his knife. Longarm kicked him so hard in the balls that the impact shot up onto his own knee.

Karl lurched forward, eyes open and mouth wide though if he said anything it was lost beneath the train noise. As the half-breed bounded off his heels toward Longarm, his eyes on fire, the lawman took one step to his left, grabbed the half-breed's collar with one hand, and heaved him out of the vestibule into open air.

There was a thud that was audible even above the roar of the iron wheels and the shriek of the wind as the big body was smacked hard by the second coach car. Karl screamed shrilly as he fell straight down on the tracks. The scream died abruptly.

When Longarm leaned out to the side to see what had

become of ole Karl, he saw only one bloody leg flying up from beneath the coach car's hammering iron wheels, and the bowie knife spinning and flashing in the afternoon sun.

When Longarm had retaken his seat and shoved his .44 Frontier Colt back into its holster, he leaned his rifle against his leg and scooped his newspaper off the floor. No one in the car appeared to have taken any notice of the dustup out in the vestibule. In fact, the baby in front of him had fallen asleep and was drooling on its mother's shoulder.

When the conductor made his way down the car and stopped to punch Longarm's ticket, the big Irishman named McInally, whom Longarm had known for years, looked around at the empty seats, frowning. "Custis, weren't there three other men sitting with you?"

"One's crow bait on the rail bed about two miles back, Lester," Longarm said, keeping his nose in his paper. "The other two're imitating cold beef sandwiches out in the vestibule yonder. Just leave 'em where they are, and I'll kick 'em over to the sheriff when we get to Pueblo."

# Chapter 4

Longarm, a rangy cowboy, and a tailless heeler named Blue were the only three passengers on the spur line's four-car combination headed toward Claireville. The conductor warned well in advance that they were approaching their destination, and that the train wouldn't stop long before it headed back the other way.

So Longarm gathered his gear and stood in the open coach door, a lit cigar wedged between his lips as he watched the dusty West Texas countryside—all brush and cactus and low, brown hills hunkered under a vast, bowl-shaped sky—roll slowly past the slow-moving, horn-blowing train. Gradually, a few mud-brick, shake-roofed shacks and stock pens slid into view among the brambles, and then the depot shuffled up before the coach car, separated from the tracks by six long, foot-wide planks cracked and bleached by the Texas sun.

The depot itself could easily have been mistaken for a mud-brick, tin-roofed chicken coop if not for its location and for the wood shingle announcing "CLAIREVILLE, SPURR COUNTY, TEXAS" extending out from its roof on wooden girders.

As the train squawked, belched, and squealed to a stop, Longarm's attention was focused on three men in front of the place. A black man and a white man sat on milk crates and played a game of checkers laid out atop a barrel between them. The third man leaned back against the wall of the depot building, ankles crossed, arms folded across his chest. All three men were shaded by the overhanging tin roof.

A dog that appeared at least half-coyote lay in the shade near the standing man, watching the train with bright, shiny eyes, tongue drooping down as it panted in the Texas heat.

"How's it look?" asked the rangy cowboy behind Longarm in the car. He looked droopy-eyed and sleep-rumpled as he climbed wearily to his feet and grabbed his single grip from the overhead storage rack.

"Like West Texas," Longarm said, looking around. "Dusty."

With that, he adjusted his saddle and war bag on his shoulder, and stepped down off the vibrating train, onto the stone-paved siding. Puffing his cheroot, he made his way across the weathered boards to the depot building, noting that both checker players as well as the gent observing them were wearing badges.

None of the three looked toward the panting train, the locomotive of which the two engineers were preparing to fill with water from the big tank along the tracks, though the white checker player said loudly enough for Longarm to hear, "Looks like the fuckin' federal from up Denver way has done arrived, Ebenezer. What do you make of that?"

The white man jumped one of the black man's checkers, and snorted a laugh. He appeared in his mid-fifties, wearing a tall Boss of the Plains Stetson, checked shirt under a brown vest and long, black duster, and batwing chaps. That he was born and raised a Texan there was no mistaking from both his dress and his thick Brazos River accent.

The black man continued staring at the checkerboard as he slowly wagged his head under a broad-brimmed black beaver hat. "Should we git up and salute the son of a bitch, or skip the formalities and git right to work polishin' his boots for him?"

He wore a bright red shirt under a black vest, with a green neckerchief and tight gray denim trousers. He had a Henry rifle draped across his thighs, and two Colts were holstered on his hips, one in the cross-draw position.

Longarm had worked with Texas lawmen before. They were a prickly lot, especially when you were working with them on their own turf. No one was as much of an outsider as a non-Texan to a Texan in Texas, be the Texan black, white, red, yellow, or cobalt blue.

Longarm dropped his saddle and war bag on the rough wooden platform, took a long puff from his cheroot, and let the smoke dribble out his nostrils. "You know, when my boss Billy Vail told me to go to hell, I didn't realize he was sending me to Texas. But now that I get here and look around, I'm wonderin' what's the fuckin' difference?"

The white lawman glanced across the checkerboard at his black opponent, then pushed himself to his feet, swinging a leg over his milk crate chair and extending a bare, calloused hand toward Longarm. He chuckled affably as he said, "Hank Tremaine at your service, sir. This here is Ranger Hall."

When Longarm had introduced himself and shaken each man's hand, he heard a scraping thump, and turned to see the third badge toter making his way around the checkerboard setup, skip-hopping on his one peg leg. He was a good-looking gent, probably in his late thirties, with humor lines around his blue eyes. He wore a blue linsey shirt, black jeans, and a red neckerchief, with an old Remington slung low on his left thigh.

"Sheriff California Todd," he said, extending a hand to Longarm. "I'm ramrod of this outfit—what there is of it. Of course, everyone knows I'm wearin' the badge because the town council's just tryin' to keep me from shootin' up the saloons like I used to do." He chuckled and pounded on the platform's half-rotten boards with his peg leg, which appeared to start just above where his right knee would have been. "Sometimes it works, sometimes it don't. But what I *can* tell you is that while these two owly sonsabitches might not be so glad to see you, I sure as hell am!"

"Why's that, Sheriff?"

"Because I'm tired of seein' my friends shot to hell. And that's what's been happenin' around here of late. Damn near as big a dustup as I saw when I was wearin' Confederate gray at Chickamauga. And it's been purty plain to me that neither the stock detectives that Pleasant Valley has called in from Fort Worth, nor"—the one-legged sheriff switched his gaze from the white checkers player to the black one—"the esteemed Texas Rangers have done one blasted thing to stop the bloodshed except to get their own killed as dead as the settlers that find themselves so unceremoniously fenced in to Pleasant Valley range."

"Ah, shit, California!" the black man intoned. "We were just on the verge of solvin' this problem before my boss called in this long, tall drink of water from up Denver way. If I told you once, I told you a thousand times, this ain't a problem we can't solve our own selves with badge toters from around here." Hall glanced sheepishly at Longarm and straightened his obviously recently brushed beaver hat. "But be that as it may, sir, we welcome you to our humble little town, and do please inform us of any way we can make you feel welcome."

"Well, for starters, you and Tremaine can quit givin' me the evil eye. And then you could direct me to a good livery where I can rent some decent horseflesh. Standin' out here palaverin' on the train platform with a couple of fuckin' overly proud Texans isn't defusing any land war, so I'd just as soon get headed out to Pleasant Valley."

Longarm hefted his saddle and war bag once more, setting both on his left shoulder while hefting his Winchester in his right hand. "Might as well start lookin' into the situation out there, since that's where the trouble began."

Sheriff California Todd hooked a thumb over his shoulder. "Only livery in town is Wainwright's, across the street. He's got about three horses for rent, and one mule, and they're probably all stolen but what can I do about it? I'm married to his daughter!"

As Longarm headed into the shabby little depot building outfitted with two church pews, a clock, a rusty woodstove, and about a half ton of dust and spiderwebs, the one-legged sheriff limped along behind him, his peg leg thumping loudly on the floor's wooden boards. The panting coyote-dog eagerly followed the sheriff, its toenails clicking frenetically.

"If you're gonna start out now, Marshal, you're gonna have to camp somewhere between here and there," Todd warned. "Pleasant Valley headquarters is nigh on a whole day's pull, though you'll be on its range only a few miles out of town."

Longarm stopped on the small boardwalk fronting the depot and facing the broad main street. There seemed to be about twelve buildings in all of Claireville—mud-brick, dusty-windowed dwellings that all leaned slightly in the same direction. They were each separated from the others by a wide gap filled with wind-jostled trash, Spanish bayo-net, and tumbleweeds. He saw two saloons directly across the wide street from each other, a church, and a single two-story hotel. The livery barn faced him.

Longarm squinted into the west-angling sun and blinked against the breeze-swept dirt and manure. The air smelled of sage, horse shit, overfilled privies, and the rotten-egg odor of an alkali creek.

"Thanks for the invitation, Sheriff," he grumbled. "But I think I'll camp in the countryside this evening."

"We'll join you, Long," said the stock detective, Tre-maine. "Old Woolyard'll be expecting us, matter of fact."

"Thanks, but I'm gonna make this a solo trip." Longarm stepped off the boardwalk, heading for the livery barn.

"I wouldn't do that if I was you, Marshal," Hall warned. "Folks out there shoot strangers on sight."

"I'll take my chances."

"All right then," Tremaine said with a mocking chuckle. "But good luck finding the headquarters. If you don't get back-shot from long range, you're liable to get good and goddamned lost. That's wide open country, and even folks with maps end up chasin' their tails over them hills."

Longarm stopped in the middle of the street. He sucked another long puff of cigar smoke, then opened his lips to let the cheroot tumble into the finely ground shit and dust, and heeled it out with his boot.

Getting lost out there in all that vast nothingness wasn't going to do him any good. Besides, the two men probably had some valuable information he'd be a fool not to glean just because they're Texans who looked at him crosswise.

"Let me get my horse," he grumbled and continued to-ward the barn.

# Chapter 5

"Care to join us, California?" asked Hank Tremaine when Longarm had picked out a blue roan stallion and was adjusting his McClellan on the horse's back.

"Now, you know I don't dare leave town that long, Hank." The handsome, peg-legged sheriff tipped his hat back off his forehead as he smiled good-naturedly up at the mounted stock detective. "What if someone robs the bank?"

"Shit."

Longarm followed Tremaine's glance to the Stockmen's Bank, which sat about forty yards east of the livery barn. The bank was another mud-brick affair that looked as wind-tortured and sun-wizened as all the other buildings in town, with a good many tumbleweeds nestled against its stone foundation. An "open" sign shone in its dusty window, but otherwise the place looked abandoned.

"I take it Claireville is still growin'," Longarm said as he swung up into his saddle.

"Or it's already done growin'," the black Ranger, Ebenezer Hall, said as he looked up and down the dusty street.

"Shit, folks came out here from the trouble farther east, had 'em one look around, and started thinkin' maybe the feudin' after the war wasn't so bad over on the Brazos side of the state."

Tremaine said, "Least it was greener over there."

"Redder, too," the sheriff said. "But now it's gettin' red over here. I wish you luck, Marshal Long." He pinched his hat brim. "You let me know if I can be of help."

"From a bar stool?" Hall said.

Todd hiked a shoulder, and he smiled good-naturedly. "I shoot better from higher ground, after I've had me a few beers."

"A few boilermakers more like," Tremaine said.

"I'll let you know what I find out," Longarm told the sheriff, feeling sorry for the man. He'd never known a one-legged man to take so much ribbing, especially from fellow lawmen. "'Spect I'll be back in a few days. A week on the outside."

With that, Longarm pinched his hat brim and reined the feisty roan westward, off the tail of Tremaine's bay and Hall's steeldust.

When he and the other two men were nearly out of town, he saw Todd limping toward a saloon on the south side of the street, where three saddle horses stood, hanging their heads. The sheriff's coyote-dog, whom Longarm had heard the sheriff call Louie, ran ahead and ducked under the batwings as though it, too, had a cold beer waiting.

Longarm turned forward. Ebenezer Hall was looking over Longarm's shoulder. He chuffed and shook his head.

"Why so hard on the man?" Longarm asked. "Ain't too many one-legged men I know with the *cajones* to wear a badge. 'Specially this far out in the tall and uncut."

"I wouldn't feel too sorry for ole California," Tremaine

said. "He comes from a rich family outta Dallas. In the War his daddy bought him a handsome position as chief adjutant to General Davis." The stock detective chuckled. "Wanna know how he got shot?"

Longarm only looked at the man riding to his right.

Tremaine glanced at Hall, who grinned, his teeth appearing unusually white inside his black goatee.

"The good general got drunk one night in their campaign tent and shot at a rat. Only it wasn't a rat. It was his young adjutant's boot. He even missed the boot, and shot ole California in the knee. Gangrene set in, and California came home to Dallas wearing only one boot."

"Christ," Longarm said. "That's a hell of a story. Kinda wished I hadn't heard it, matter o' fact."

"That ain't the end of it. Him and his folks—moneyed people from Alabama, don't ya know—got caught up in the feuds after the War. They sided with the carpetbaggers, sorta kissed their Northern asses to keep their banking business, though they're every bit as Confederate as they were *before* the War. Well, California's old man got himself shot in a duel with a man named Chaz Doolittle, a hotel owner from Tennessee, over the affections of one black soiled dove in downtown Dallas. Doolittle was still a proud old Reb. Well, neither family liked the outcome, and all hell broke loose. Quite a dustup. Many brothers and cousins, even friends, on both sides got killed.

"So California—who never really did take part in the fight 'cause he didn't have the stomach for it—came runnin' out here to save his skin, hopin' for a little peace and quiet. Turns out the manager of the Pleasant Valley outfit knew California's old man and pretty much got him the job o' county sheriff without even goin' through the pomp and circumstance of a local election."

"Still sounds to me like he's had his share of hard luck," Longarm said. "And he *is* wearin' the badge."

Holding his reins high as he turned his horse around a rock in the trail, Tremaine said, "The point is he comes from money, and he did everything he could to stay outta harm's way during the War. He comes out here, and he's still gettin' gold nuggets handed to him in a silk sack. Spends most of his time collectin' his pay from a bar stool."

"Yeah, but he pays every night he goes home to that mouse-faced, black-hearted little gal of his," Hall laughed. "There was another bit of bad luck he didn't see comin'!"

"Yeah, but she sees *him* comin'," Tremaine said. "Every night, she sees him comin' home drunk from the Bluebonnet Saloon, and, boy, don't ya know she makes him pay!"

The Texans laughed.

Longarm only looked from one man to the other and clamped his hat down tighter on his head.

He'd been to Texas a few times in the past, after the war, but things were even more divided than he'd thought. Animosity ran high, and an outsider like him would have to spend a couple years down here to even begin to fathom all the feuding motivations. Part of it, he knew, stemmed from the fact that most Texans had originated in the clannish South, where it didn't take much provocation to pit a family from one hollow against a family from another. They'd brought all that hot blood to Texas, and after the war that powder keg was shoved even closer to the bonfire.

A few miles west of Claireville, the three riders turned off the main trail onto a horse trail that forked northward. They soon came to a barbed-wire fence stretching off over the dun, scrubby hills to the west and east.

"Damn," Longarm said. He had the old frontiersman's

natural aversion to the confining, deadly "bobwire" invented by Joseph Glidden a few years back, in '73. The
nasty barbs on the wire sparked in the light of the west-
falling sun, glistening like tiny stilettos. "I take it this is the
boundary of Pleasant Valley."

"Sure as shit," Hall said as he dismounted to open the
Texas gate. "If I had a penny for every acre old Woolyard
has covered under this here devil wire, I could retire and
whore away the rest of my years in New Orleans."

He opened the gate, and they rode through.


The trio followed one meandering horse trail after another,
along the sides of hills and over them, over saddleback
ridges and through dry washes.

Longarm hadn't ridden far from Claireville before he
felt damn glad the stock detective and the Ranger—as la-
conic and obviously territorial as they both were—had
ridden along to point the way to the Pleasant Valley headquarters. If there was a main, marked trail, Longarm saw no
sign of one. Of course the Texans might be showing him a
roundabout way just for shits and giggles, but they seemed
to be making a beeline toward the northwest, which was,
according to the directions included in the papers Vail had
provided, where the headquarters was located, about fifty
miles from Claireville.

It was a vast expanse of low, rolling hills covered with
chalky dirt and sand and pocked with tough, wiry brush,
some of which Longarm recognized as dog cactus, sage,
willow, with here and there a yucca or an agave plant.
Prickly pear was almost everywhere, and the horse trails,
spotted with dried apples, meandered around such dangerous, spiny patches.

In the far northwest, the Guadalupe Mountains hovered

just above the lemon-green desert and the far horizon, blue as storm clouds.

Longarm pumped Hall and Tremaine for information and received only cryptic answers, mostly in the form of grunts, until he asked who they thought was responsible for Pleasant Valley's primary stock loss.

"Aside from the dry summers," Hall said, "Woolyard thinks the main culprit's the Wolf Creek spread. It's wedged in a big canyon about thirty miles west of the Pleasant Valley headquarters, on a big sprawl of school land. Old greaser named Miguel Corpus runs the place. Claims his land was granted to his family by the king of Spain, but the courts disagree."

"You boys have had a talk with old Corpus, have you?"

"Tried," Tremaine said, "but since Woolyard sent night riders to his place, and wounded a couple of his men in a shootin' scrape, the old man lets no one near. Shoots first and asks questions later. Can't blame him, I reckon."

They crested a low rise, with a vast flat stretching ahead of them, relieved now and then by low rimrocks that were darkening now as the sun hovered close to the western horizon. Tremaine chewed off a hunk from a tobacco twist and continued: "But Woolyard's lost several men out there, toward Corpus's Wolf Creek range. Some he's found nestling with the sand rattlers. Others just disappeared . . . along with a good quarter of his whole projected increase in herd numbers over the last two years."

"Plenty of small-time rustlers out here, too," Hall said, riding lazily on the far side of the stock detective. "Lots of places for 'em to hole up, lots of places to hide good-sized stolen herds."

"Woolyard's always had problems with rustlers up from Mexico or down from Oklahoma," Tremaine said, chewing with his mouth open and breathing loudly through his nose. "But what we got goin' on now is a big cattle-thievin' operation. Well organized, with a good number of men. My bet is it's old Corpus, but since we ain't been able to git close . . . and then your boss, Marshal Vail from up Denver way, coaxed us all to cool our heels . . ."

He gave Longarm a sneering glance as he let his voice trail off.

"I know, I know," Longarm said. "Otherwise, you'd have the trouble cleaned up by now."

"Most likely," Tremaine grunted.

"Or we'd be damn close leastways," Hall said.

Longarm glanced at the black Ranger. "How is it your captain trusts you not to go off half-cocked out here, like the other Rangers on his roll? Don't you have no relatives around here? No stake?"

"Nah," Hall said. "Unlike most of the boys in our troop, I'm from New Orleans. I just come out here for the dry air." He pressed a fist to his chest. "Helps with my asthma, don't ya know."

"But you still don't care for my interference, that it?"

"That's pretty much it, Marshal. I'm a Ranger, ya see? There ain't no trouble in Texas we Rangers can't solve— given enough leeway, that is."

"Leeway," Longarm grunted as he dropped down toward a water hole among rocks and wiry willow shrubs. "I reckon with enough leeway, we lawdogs would all have a far easier time of it. Trouble is, when that happens, it gets kinda hard to tell who's the law and who's *against* it."

Longarm swung down from his saddle to let his horse drink from the cool, dark water bubbling up from the mossy rocks. When the other two men had watered their own mounts, they continued northwest in the same, testy silence that had marked most of the ride from Claireville so far.

An hour after they'd left the water hole, good dark came down, and a chill wind came up. Fast-moving clouds blotted out the stars.

"Ah, shit," Ranger Hall said. "I don't like the sound of this."

There *was* a sound, too. A raspy, far-off howling like that which a distant but fast-approaching train makes.

Longarm hauled back on the roan's reins. Lightning flashed straight ahead of him and low to the ground. The wind whipped dirt up around him, and it was like getting peppered with buckshot. The horse nickered, then whinnied, shaking its head.

The chugging noise grew louder. Longarm could feel the ground vibrating up through his horse and into his saddle.

The other riders' horses whinnied and skitter-hopped.

"Ah, fuck!" Hall shouted. "*Cyclone!*"

As one, all three men reined their horses around and heeled them back the way they'd come. A hundred yards along their backtrail they'd skirted a limestone shelf jutting up from a hogback, and it was this they headed for now.

The wind churned up the sand, cactus spines, and other grit and blew it against the men and the horses. It was a muggy wind, and it smelled musty, as though a door had been thrown wide on a long-sealed cellar. Rain began to spit down at a slant from the dark sky, and thunder rumbled.

Longarm followed Hall down a slope and sharply left to the backside of the shelf. Tremaine galloped behind him. All three dismounted in a hurry and, clutching their horse's reins, climbed a sandy rise to hunker low behind the shelf's base.

Beyond the shelf, that metaphorical train was now screaming and hammering. The air swirled atop the shelf, and Longarm had to suck hard to get breath into his lungs, while gripping his terrified horse's reins with one hand and holding his hat on his head with the other.

From somewhere inside the wind there sounded something strange—like the bellow of some frightened beast.

"What the hell's that?" Longarm shouted.

"Cow!" Tremaine shouted back. "Wind's got him. He'll prob'ly be in New Mexico come mornin'."

Longarm pulled his hat down low on his forehead and pressed his shoulder tight against the stone shelf.

He jerked his head up when he heard another bizarre, tooth-gnashing sound, like a man's scream, beneath the hammering, howling wind.

Longarm and the other two men shared a horrified glance.

"Damn," Hall said, his chocolate eyes wide. "I sure hope that waddie has wings!"

# Chapter 6

When the tornado had passed off to the east like a pack of howling, snarling demon-hounds, the rain started in earnest, driving down at a slant and instantly turning the shelf above the three lawmen into a series of cascading waterfalls.

Witches' fingers of lightning snaked out of the weathery darkness, flashing, crackling, and popping, filling the air with the smell of brimstone. Thunder roared like boulders being hurled straight down from heaven by a piss-burned god at the final end of his tether.

The three lawmen found a hollow in the stony dike, hastily erected a lean-to over the top, and hunkered inside the inadequate shelter in silent discomfort, the storm raising such a ruckus that it would have been impossible to hold a conversation had they been so inclined, which they weren't.

When the rain abated, they unsaddled their skittish, nerve-exhausted mounts and hunkered down to sleep the wretched sleep of the soaked. It was a long, uncomfortable night, and at dawn the next morning, the men, chilled to the bone in their still wet clothes and snarling at one another like rabid coyotes, saddled up after only a few bites of jerky for sustenance. There was no dry wood anywhere around for a fire. Rainwater still dripped from the stone shelf, and rivulets trickled everywhere, cutting their way to widely scattered arroyos.

Mounting up and reining their horses out from behind the stone shelf, the sun just now turning the eastern horizon a vivid rose, with small gray birds flitting here and there about the scrub and singing happily, the grim lawmen resumed their trek northward through the now-soggy but fragrant West Texas desert.

"I'd give my right nut for a hot cup of bellywash," Hall grunted.

It was the only thing that any of the three muttered until, two hours later, they pulled rein to stare down at the body of a dead man lying slumped at the base of a blood-smeared boulder.

"I'll be goddamned," Tremaine said. "Poor bastard didn't have wings, after all."

As he looked down at the dead man, Longarm's empty guts twitched and his lips twisted themselves into a grimace. Last night's wind had apparently blown the man's shirt off and ripped his underwear shirt down to his waist, exposing his pale, slightly hairy chest and paunch. It had ripped his jeans down around his ankles. One boot was gone, and the other appeared to have been about to come off before the cyclone had dropped the poor bastard here, smashing him off the boulder and letting him pile up here at its base. His skull was split wide, and brain and blood painted the side of the rock, drying in the hot, morning sun.

Though the man was dead, Longarm felt guilty for looking at him in his undignified state, jeans pulled down as though he'd been about to take a private shit when the wind had so unceremoniously taken him for a long, last ride.

"Here's his horse," Hall said. He'd ridden to the far side of the boulder and climbed a low hill beyond. "Guts're spillin' out." The black man made a retching sound. "Damn, that's an awful smell!"

Longarm and the other two men decided to spend an hour here, burying the dead man and building a fire to dry themselves out and to make breakfast. It was while scouring the brush for dry wood—it apparently hadn't rained as hard here as it had farther south—that they found several cows lying smashed and dead in the scrub. The drover had obviously been herding the stock when the cyclone grabbed them all.

When they'd dried their clothes around the fire, eaten some biscuits and side pork, and drank some badly needed java, the three men mounted once more and continued north, leaving the freshly mounded grave marked by a makeshift cross behind them, amongst the agave, the lime-green sage, and the already bloating corpses of four cows and a horse.

All the stock wore the Bar-V brand of the Pleasant Valley Ranch.

Longarm was silently exclaiming his awe at the size of the Pleasant Valley spread, for the ninth or tenth time that morning, when a red, peaked roof rose up against the horizon before him, perched atop a broad, dun-colored hill. Ebenezer Hall had just stuck his arm out to point, when three rifle reports sounded, flattening out across the broad bowl the three riders were in.

Hall jerked his hand to his revolver, as did Longarm and Tremaine, though none of the three so much as unsnapped the keeper thongs over their gun hammers. Jerking back on his roan's reins with his left hand, Longarm looked in the direction of the shots and saw a rider standing atop a hill about a hundred yards away. The man wore a high-crowned hat, and he held his rifle in one hand, straight up in the air high above his head.

Longarm kept a gloved hand curled around his Colt's polished walnut grip. The shots had likely been a warning signal to him, Hall, and Tremaine, as well as to the big, red-roofed house atop the far northern hill.

"We best wait here," Tremaine said.

He and Hall had stopped their mounts to Longarm's left, on the two-track trail they'd picked up about hour ago. "Let 'em get a good gander at us, so's we don't git shot out of our saddles. Ole Woolyard's got his men on high alert, looks like. Wonder what the hell's been goin' on past few weeks."

"I don't know, but he's got us hemmed in purty good," Longarm said, looking around.

Two riders headed toward them from behind. Three had seemingly materialized from the sage and Spanish bayonet to the west and were loping their horses toward the new-comers, hatted heads bobbing, the thumps of their mounts' hooves gradually growing audible.

The signal shooter sat his steeldust atop the far eastern hill, his rifle barrel bristling up from his lap as he stared toward the three newcomers, waiting. Presently, three riders appeared cresting a hill below the big house ahead. One rode slightly in front of the other two, and Longarm saw long hair bouncing on narrow shoulders, beneath the brim of a green, billed, English-style riding hat. As the three approached, Longarm's lips quirked skeptically.

Hall muttered, "Hold on to your balls, gents. The she-bitch who guards the gates of hell is here, her own self."

The three riders from the ranch headquarters drew rein, the girl's high-stepping black Thoroughbred snorting and shaking its head, the sun flashing off its own copper eyes as well as the green ones of its golden-haired rider.

"Afternoon, Miss Verna," Tremaine said, pinching his hat brim. "Where your pa?"

"I'll do the askin' here, Mr. Tremaine. Who's this?" The girl's sharp eyes drilled Longarm like Apache war lances, her long, wavy blond hair blowing back from her oval-shaped, peaches-and-cream face with its long, straight nose and pointed, dimpled chin. She spoke in a faint English accent. Her horse pranced and skitter-hopped.

Tremaine opened his mouth to speak, but Longarm cut him off. "Deputy U.S. Marshal Custis Long, at your service, ma'am. Miss Woolyard, I presume?"

"It's about time you got here," the girl said in her biting, angry tone. But all the scowling in the world couldn't take the beauty from her heavenly features. "The cease-fire is off. Come on up to the house, and my father will explain why!"

Longarm shared a dark glance with the other two men. The girl neck-reined her spry stallion, batted her heels against its ribs, and headed back in the direction from which she and her two sullen, well-armed, hard-eyed co-horts had ridden.

Longarm put his own horse forward, as did Tremaine and Hall.

As they mounted the first hill toward the red-roofed lodge, Longarm cast a glance across his backtrail. The riders behind fell back, scattering. So did those in the west. The man who'd fired the warning shots had already disappeared, likely returning to his sentinel post.

The main headquarters of the Pleasant Valley Ranch rose and shifted on the broad hilltop in front of Longarm. As he'd expected from a company that had claimed half a

million West Texas acres spread across three counties, it
was no modest affair.

There were at least three barns that Longarm could see,
a half dozen corrals with stock chutes and snubbing posts,
hay sheds, windmills, and sundry other adobe-brick and
wood-frame outbuildings, including what was obviously
the bunkhouse. It was a vast, L-shaped affair, with a couple
of saddle horses lazing at the hitch rack out front. Smoke
skeined from a sandstone chimney. A cowboy in dusty
chaps and a black Stetson was adjusting the stirrups on one
of the horses as he narrowed his eyes at the three newcomers riding past the bunkhouse, behind the girl and the two
sullen riders who flanked her like overprotective body-
guards.

A half dozen other men milled about the corrals and
blacksmith shop, and there was the echoing clatter of a
smithy's hammer. But a brooding, ominous quiet was almost palpable here. Far different from most of the ranches
Longarm had visited, where there was almost always an air
of joking and easy laughter in spite of the hard work that
went on nearly twenty-four hours a day.

The trail to the main lodge climbed a bench as it continued a good hundred yards beyond the work buildings. Several dogs ran out from beneath the broad front porch to
bark and raise their hackles or wag their tails at the new-
comers, then to get sidetracked by a skirmish among themselves. Longarm drew rein with the others in front of the
main lodge, raking his eyes from the willowy, curvy form
of the blond Woolyard girl as she lithely dismounted her
frisky stallion, to admire the house itself.

The lodge was three stories of weathered pink adobe
fashioned in the Mexican style, with broad galleries jutting
from all three floors. The galleries were wood, painted a

green that stood out against the pink walls and the ochre of the tiled roof. On the galleries were hanging potted plants, a couple of statues of saints likely gleaned from old, abandoned cemeteries, and the hammered steel breastplate, helmet, and sword of a Spanish conquistador.

The two men who'd ridden down the hill with the girl tied their stock ponies to one of the three hitch racks fronting the place, while Longarm, Tremaine, and Hall tied theirs to another. The girl tied hers to the rack nearest the front door. There was the sudden, raucous rasp of a rifle breech being levered opened and closed. It echoed from inside the open, arched front door, along with a loud thumping sound, not unlike that of the strenuous maneuverings of the peg-legged sheriff back in Claireville— California Todd.

Only the man who appeared in the lodge's front door was considerably larger and older and more grizzled than Todd. And instead of hobbling on a false leg, this man was on two crutches. His bulbous-nosed face was brick-red, setting off the iron-gray of his thick, curly hair and muttonchop whiskers.

"Who the fuck is it?" he bellowed in a heavy Scottish accent as he bulled through the opening, shifting one crutch and then the other and appearing reluctant to put much weight on either of his knee-high, lace-up boots.

"That federal lawdog the Rangers sent for, Papa," said the girl, swinging around to confront Longarm and his two partners. "He's finally arrived." She curled her lip with disapproval as she added, "Along with Misters Tremaine and Hall."

"'Bout goddamn time you got here!" Woolyard exclaimed as he thumped out to the edge of the porch and stared down the steps, his gray-blue eyes sparking like ice from their deep, red, leathery sockets. "I've called off the truce! Sure as clover in County Kerry, I have, and it's a bloody time in Pleasant Valley!"

"When did you do that, Mr. Woolyard?" Longarm asked, shifting his eyes back to the lovely blonde who stood with one black boot on the gallery's bottom step. She wore a red-and-blue striped, collarless shirt, and her breasts jutted invitingly albeit haughtily. "And *why*, if you don't mind me askin', sir?"

"'Cause me and several of my men were ambushed a few days back, out on the Trinidad flats. In broad daylight, six riders come stormin' out of the caprock, blastin' away like they thought it was your War Between the Fuckin' States all over again. Killed two of my men. Shot my horse out from under me. Then as I was climbing to my feet and reaching for my rifle, one of them drilled a blue whistler through me bloody *arse*!"

Tremaine glanced quickly, wryly at Hall, who did not return the look. The black man held the gaze of the old, hairy, fiery-eyed Scot glaring down at them all from atop the gallery.

Woolyard tossed his head, with its cap of tangled curls, toward the door behind him and swung around, clomping and stomping on his crutches. "Get in here, gentlemen!"

He headed for the door. He wasn't wearing a coat—only canvas trousers and a deerskin shirt. One of his trousers' big hip pockets showed a large, red, ragged-edged stain.

"Oh, Papa!" the girl intoned, remaining at the bottom of the stairs. "You've opened your stitches again with all your carryin' on!"

"Don't pester me, girl!" the old man said, his voice booming as he entered the house. "I got no time for cater-waulin' females. This is *war*!"

Longarm started up the steps behind Tremaine and Hall. He paused and gestured for the girl to head in before him. Inadvertently, his eyes dropped to her heaving bosom. She was a full-breasted girl despite her willowy frame. For just a half wink of vaguely conscious time as he drew her feminine scent into his nostrils, he couldn't help imagining her writhing naked beneath him.

She must have seen it in his eyes. They sparked and narrowed, and she hardened her jaws as she growled, "After *you*, sir!"

# Chapter 7

Not long after they were seated in the high-ceilinged, heavy-beamed parlor of the Pleasant Valley Ranch's main lodge, each man with a drink of Woolyard's barn-brewed hooch in his fist, the rancher turned to Longarm and announced with no small air of defiance that he was going to hunt down the men who had bushwhacked him and lynch them, and there wasn't a damn thing Longarm could do about it.

Longarm sipped his drink. It wasn't as good as his Maryland rye, but it wasn't half-bad. He took a deep puff off a fresh three-for-a-nickel cheroot and held the Scotsman's openly challenging, self-satisfied stare.

"I appreciate your bluntness, Mr. Woolyard," the lawman said. "Now appreciate this: You send any men out heeled for war, and if you accost anyone you don't know for double-damn sure was part of the group that pinked your English ass, I'm gonna throw the cuffs on ya. I'm gonna haul you back to Claireville and throw your aching ass in the hoosegow until this matter is done settled."

Tremaine and Hall both turned to Longarm, their eyes

wide. Verna Woolyard, the comely daughter who'd been placing a tray of smoked meat and cheese on a low table, turned to Longarm and gasped, narrowing her eyes again with exasperation.

Woolyard kept his eyes on Longarm's. They flashed slightly. One lid twitched.

"You're bluffing, sir."

"I wouldn't bet on it."

"How would you propose to get me through my men, Deputy Long? I have twenty-two still on my roll despite tornadoes, lightning, drought, and murder. And every one I have is nastier than a frying pan full of diamondbacks, and none wouldn't hesitate to kill a federal lawman . . . if I gave the order."

Longarm slid his double-action .44 from his holster and set the butt on his knee. He ratcheted the hammer back and angled the barrel toward the Scot's flat belly. The click echoed off the fireplace to the lawman's right, which was big enough to roast two good-sized javelinas simultaneously, and rolled straight up toward the second-floor and third-floor wraparound balconies high above.

The girl gasped again, straightening her back as she turned toward the surly guest.

Longarm rolled his cigar to the other side of his mouth. "I have cuffs, to boot. If you still think I'm bluffing, I'll hog-tie you right now, this very minute. I'll throw you— sore ass and all—over the back of one of your own good horses and lead you out of here. If any of your men so much as glance at a weapon, I'll drill you through an arm, and I'll continue perforating your hide until I get a clear path back to town. If I got nothin' livin' to turn the key on, so much the better. Half my job settlin' this feud will be done, then, won't it?"

Woolyard lowered his eyes to the cocked gun in Longarm's hand. He lifted them again to the lawman's iron-solid gaze. Verna Woolyard stood statue-still, delicate jaw hanging, green eyes suddenly wary, cautious, as though she were suddenly realizing she'd stumbled into a wolf den.

Tremaine and Hall shifted their own bright, bemused gazes between Longarm and the owly Scot.

A silence stretched, taut as razor wire. There was only the sound of the hot breeze working at the corners of the giant house, and the distant, intermittent rings of the blacksmith's hammer.

"You wouldn't," Verna said softly, breathless, eyes darting between Longarm's implacable face and the cocked Colt resting on his knee.

"He would indeed," Woolyard said, his tone bemused.

The old Scot laughed, his eyes now cast with admiration.

"Sure as hellfire in a pool of screamin' sinners, the good deputy is not bluffing. I have a feelin', dear Verna, he might be a man to ride the river with, even climb a mountain or two." Woolyard threw his head back and laughed with delight. "All right, I defer to the federal lawman," he told Longarm.

Tremaine and Hall eased back in their seats. The color returned to Verna's smooth cheeks.

"You may holster your hogleg, Mr. Long," Woolyard said. "I'll give you ten days to find out who's responsible for my steadily dwindling herds and bring them to your own, official brand of justice. If you haven't run them to ground by then, I get my turn."

Longarm depressed the Colt's hammer and lifted the barrel. "Fine as frog hair."

He twirled the gun on his finger—somewhat shamelessly showing off for the girl—then slid it back into its holster. He snapped the keeper thong closed, drew a deep-lunged puff of cheap tobacco smoke, removed the cheroot from his teeth, and blew the smoke at the ceiling.

"Now, then, Mr. Woolyard, I hope we can hoof it on over to more useful topics of conversation, such as the exact whereabouts of the other day's shoot-out. With luck, I might be able to cut the bushwhackers' sign and track them to their lair. Looking at a fairly detailed map of the Pleasant Valley holdings would make my job a whole lot easier."

"I doubt you'll cut their sign. They headed into the lava bluffs. Might as well try to track a snake across a windy lake. But it's that greaser Corpus's men, I'm sure. Be that as it may . . . your hand, my dear." Woolyard winced as he shifted his sore ass in his overstuffed leather seat and threw his arm up toward his daughter.

His mood seemed a half-ton lighter than when Longarm and the other two visitors had first ridden up to the house, and Longarm thought he should maybe start pulling his hogleg more often. Seemed to make folks a whole lot more cooperative.

"The best map is in my office. Ranger Hall, grab the hooch, will you? We'll change rooms and then take our supper in the dining room yonder."

When the girl had him standing and hobbling toward an arched doorway, Longarm and the others following, the Scot squeezed his daughter's shoulder and said, "Verna, tell Tio we'll have the porterhouse this evening. And dust off a bottle of that Spanish brandy I brought back from Chicago. Do you men like to gamble? I haven't gambled with sporting fellows in a month of fuckin' Sundays!"

He laughed, then grabbed his ass, dropped a crutch, nearly fell, and cursed.

After their stare-down in the lodge's main parlor, Longarm and Woolyard got along famously the whole rest of the night. There was an air of celebration about the house, in fact, and several of the Scot's top hands were brought in to partake in the festivities, which included a succulent porterhouse steak served by Woolyard's Mexican cook and by the still-owly and obviously disapproving Miss Verna, with all the trimmings, including dessert and coffee.

After dessert, the men quit the dining room for the two baize-covered tables in Woolyard's personal gambling parlor and library. The book-lined room was appointed with game trophies; maps of the U.S., Britain, and even Africa, where Woolyard had hunted big game; and nearly every weapon Longarm could name, and a good many he couldn't. Soon the air was so thick with billowing clouds of tobacco smoke that the lawman, accustomed to the rowdiest perdition dens in Denver, had to hold his cards up close to his face to read the suits.

The only thing Longarm didn't like about the evening's ebb toward gambling and general male high jinks was that it didn't include Miss Verna. It was obvious she had no use for his law-bringing intrusion into what she considered her father's affairs, but he found her ripe, smooth-cheeked, full-busted presence a thrill just the same.

Woolyard, drunk as a lord and singing at the top of his lungs, turned in around midnight, as even a boatload of brandy and sherry hadn't totally dulled the pain in his ass. The rest of the men soon followed, Longarm, Tremaine, and Hall being shown to their second- and third-story rooms by the Mexican cook who doubled as Woolyard's housekeeper.

Longarm's own room was on the third story, its two windows overlooking the northern, star-capped range from which the occasional bellow of a lonesome cow sounded, and the yammering of hunting coyotes. A bobcat hide covered the double bed, which boasted large oak posts and a stout headboard with the Pleasant Valley brand burned into it by a hot running iron. The other furnishings were simple but comfortable, and an old Hawken blunderbuss, like what the trappers used a half century ago, with the name James R. Woolyard engraved in the scarred stock, rested on stout spikes over the heavy timbered door.

Apparently, Horace Woolyard of Pleasant Valley wasn't the first Woolyard to visit the American West.

His head reeling from more liquor than he should have imbibed—he had a big ride ahead of him tomorrow, in hopes of cutting the ambushers' sign—Longarm removed his pistol rig and shell belt, dropped them on a chair, shrugged out of his frock coat, and plopped down heavily on the edge of the big, thick-mattressed bed.

A muffled, high-pitched yawn sounded.

Pinching a cold, half-smoked cheroot between his teeth, Longarm looked around. Had the yawn come from the hall? He started to rise, and there was a low, wooden squeak that had not come from the hall but from behind him.

He turned to find a second door in the opposite wall from the hall door. He moved to the second door, tripped the small, steel locking bolt, and opened it. The door opened onto an outside balcony overlooking the lodge's night-cloaked backyard, from which the collective screech of insects sounded above the intermittent bellowing of distant cattle, like the beat of a giant heart.

A lamp glowed to his left. He turned toward it.

Someone gasped.

Longarm's right cheek twitched with a start, and he found his right hand snaking across his belly toward the .44 that was no longer riding high on his left hip. Remembering that he'd left the pistol rig on the chair, he stayed his hand.

"Pardon *me*!" A girl's voice said from somewhere in the gauzy, bronze-tinted shadows beneath the hurricane lantern that hung from the adobe wall over a wooden bench.

There was the wooden creak again, and then Longarm saw a long, creamy leg and a bare, feminine foot extending out from under the hem of a blue silk nightdress. Up closer to the light, two full mounds shone beneath the nightdress's low, lace-edged neck, divided by deep, shaded cleavage. Above the cleavage, the lantern revealed a light salting of tiny freckles. Slowly, one arm swept a thick, green blanket across the breasts, keeping the cover low enough, however, that the dark, mysterious cleavage remained bare—deep and dusky with erotic allure.

Slowly, the girl's left leg, bare from mid-thigh down— oh, what a tender stretch of the smooth, porcelain flesh of inner thigh just above the knee and beneath her hidden crotch!—was folded beneath the other and tucked up securely beneath the dress.

Longarm's gaze found the girl's eyes, burning like twin amethysts in the desert sun, just beneath the lantern. "No, I reckon it's pardon me," he drawled as he continued on out the door. "Hope I ain't interruptin'."

He fished a lucifer from his shirt pocket, scratched it to life on the scarred rail, and fired his half-smoked cheroot.

The girl said tightly, "As you can see, you *are*. I came out here for some air before I turned in for the evenin'."

Puffing his cheroot, Longarm glanced at the open door just beyond the girl's head, and her blond hair fanned about her shoulders and glowing in the lantern's buttery light. "That your room yonder?"

"It is. Don't tell me Tio put you in there . . . in the room . . . well, in the room next to *mine*!"

"Indeed, he did. Ain't that a damn coincidence?"

"Well . . . I . . . I'm very sorry, Deputy Long, but Tio has made a mistake. I usually reserve the third floor for my-self."

"Why is that, Miss Verna?"

She stared at him. The skin above her nose wrinkled. "Why is what?"

"Why do you reserve the whole third floor for yourself, in a house as big as this one?"

"Why, for privacy, of course. I am a lone female out here, Deputy Long, amongst all these men . . . these . . . *misfits*!"

Longarm turned to the night, took a deep drag off the ci-gar, and removed it from his lips. "Must get kinda lonely. A girl out here . . . all alone amongst these misfits."

Longarm felt her eyes on him. He thought he could see the green of them flashing in the slightly guttering lantern light.

"What are you getting at, Deputy?"

"I'm sayin' why the charade?" Longarm turned to her. "If you want a man to grease your wheels and blow the dust from your smokestacks, just come out and say it." He moved to her, dropped his hand to her calf. She sat frozen as he slid his hand beneath the hem of her nightdress and began sliding it and the dress slowly up the long, smooth length of her leg.

"But first," he grinned, "you're gonna have to say it."

# Chapter 8

Longarm had only to remove his hand from the girl's thigh before she said: "Okay!"

She wallowed, staring up at him, reaching for his hand and replacing it on the tenderness of her thigh, which was as unblemished as freshly sanded and varnished oak, and the color of ivory. "You've found me out for what I am—a harlot. Just touch me, and keep touching me, Deputy Long. That's all I ask."

"Since we're so close of a sudden, you might as well call me Longarm, I reckon."

"All right. Longarm." Verna Woolyard hesitated, her thigh quivering slightly under his rough palm. "Do you think me depraved?"

"Well, you're tricky—that's for damn sure," Longarm said, sliding his hand up until the side of it touched the curly hair of her crotch and detected the slight moistness there. "You might've just said what you wanted, instead of acting all uppity and . . . mad."

"It's just that . . . I didn't really know what I wanted. I mean, deep down I guess I did. And I guess it made me sort

of angry at you . . . for temping me so terribly. You see . . ."
She sobbed, gritted her teeth, and closed both her hands
over his, grinding his fingers into her wetness. "Oh, god,
you don't know how lonely I've been out here, Longarm!"

It didn't take him long to fully understand just how
lonely the girl obviously was. Or, if not lonely, at least love
hungry. Although she had strategically placed his room next
to hers on the otherwise vacant third story and on the opposite side of the house from her father's room on the second
story, Longarm carried her into the privacy of his own
room. He kicked the door closed and, on a drunken whim,
set her on the first piece of furniture he came to—a tall,
stout chest of drawers, the top of which was about even
with his mustache.

She shrieked with pleasure and wriggled her bottom
around atop the chest as she hiked her nightgown up her
thighs, exposing the V of blond hair at her crotch. Longarm
leaned forward and rammed his nose into her snatch, which
she'd obviously prepared for him, as it smelled like wild
cherry blossoms and talcum. He scrounged around in there
with nose, tongue, and mustache until he had her fairly
convulsing with pleasure and tugging painfully at his hair.

When he had her as ripe as a summer cantaloupe, he
carried her over to the bed and laid her down on her back,
her knees raised and her feet spread. He kicked his boots
off, shucked out of his clothes, and mounted the mewling,
fair little damsel from Scotland. He impaled her with his
throbbing dong, burying it so deep he thought he could feel
her heart heaving against its swollen head, and gave her a
good and proper fucking that nearly broke the bed.

When they'd both recovered, she got down on her hands
and knees on the floor, and wagged her ass.

"Come on, Custis," she raspily urged, throwing her hair

down her slender, curving back. "Let's do it dirty, and then I'll let you sleep and get all rested up for your investigation tomorrow."

Longarm couldn't believe he could get it up a second time, after all the liquor he'd consumed downstairs and after his first bout between Verna's trembling knees. But when he looked from the girl's flushed and sweaty ass to his own crotch, sure enough, his shaft was as hard as the rear axle of a Conestoga freight wagon. He ran his fingers through his sweat-damp hair, then dropped to his knees behind the girl.

"Wait!" She turned suddenly, facing him on her knees.

She pumped his cock a few times, then, giving him a coy look through those eyes as green as the Scottish hills, she lowered her head to the throbbing member. She extended her pink tongue, and continuing to stare up at him, her expression now so different from that which she'd favored him with all night, she tilted her head to one side and licked his full, engorged length, from the scrotum to the pee hole at the tip of its purple head.

"Ummm . . . scrumptious!" she said, smacking her lips. "Okay!"

She turned and rammed her pink ass against his dong, dropping her elbows to the floor. Her back made a perfect sloping trough from her round white rump to the thick swirls of blond hair fanned out across her shoulders. Longarm grabbed his cock in his right fist and slid himself into the girl's steaming, sopping portal.

"Oh," she said as he began thrusting. "Oh . . . that's. . . . that's just *dreamy*!"

When he was through, he damn near passed out on the girl's back. She was slumped forward, tits-down against the floor. With effort, he hauled himself upright, his chest sticking slightly to her back, and, rising, he wrapped an arm around her waist and lifted her up, as well. She groaned. Her hair flew out from her back as, wheeling, he flung her carelessly onto the bed, where she bounced several times, groaning and drawing her knees up.

"Oh," she said, breathless. "You're a rough bastard, aren't you?"

Longarm flopped down on his back beside her. "You oughta be used to that. Plenty of rough bastards out here, aren't there?" He suspected that she hadn't kept this isolated room just to entertain one visitor she hadn't even known was coming. She must have invited a few of her father's men up a time or two in the past.

"Yes, I guess I am, but I take exception with what you're intimating, Custis."

"You tryin' to tell me none of them . . . ?"

"That's exactly what I'm telling you. I took this room because I get headaches sometimes and can't stand the noise from the main yard. All that clanging from the blacksmith shop an' such. About drives me to hang myself from the nearest tree."

Verna propped herself on her elbow, snuggling up close to Longarm's long frame, and buried the thumb and index finger of her left hand in his chest hair. "I can't say that I haven't been tempted, a time or two. I do have my needs, like any other nineteen-year-old girl."

She leaned forward and gave his lips a sensuous nibble. "I was raised in Edinburgh, you see, and came out here just last year, when my mother died. Mother came out here only once, when Father first came six years ago to manage the ranch for the company. After two weeks, she deemed western Texas fit for only coyotes and cactus, and took me back to Scotland, and put me in an art and music school. So, you see, I'm used to more inspiring surroundings and"—she allowed herself a small, devilish smile as she rubbed Longarm's side with her nose— "gentlemen callers."

Longarm ran a hand through the girl's silky hair. "There wasn't anyone back home you coulda stayed with?"

Verna shook her head. "Mother's clan disowned her when she married a Woolyard. And, well, Father's clan disowned him."

"When he married your mother." Longarm shook his head. "Damn, you're in a pickle here, girl."

"Oh, it's not so bad." Verna ran her hand across Longarm's washboard belly, tracing the ribbed muscles with her finger. "I get along. I ride my horse, Indigo, and I paint and play the piano downstairs for Father. Tio's getting too old and rickety to handle all the cleaning, and I'm glad to help out. Gives me something to do."

"Old Tio must be a little suspicious, ain't he?" Longarm said, looking around the lamp-lit room. "About you ordering me so close . . . ?"

She chuckled and dipped her fingers down toward his slumbering member. Tired as he was, Longarm felt a tingle down there. "Tio's Mexican," Verna said, her voice low with meaning. "He knows how it is for me. He won't say a word to Papa. In fact, Papa thinks you've been quartered with Mr. Tremaine and Ranger Hall."

She gave a girlish giggle and coiled herself like a snake against Longarm. She placed her hand over his cock, and looked up at him, the corners of her mouth rising, her green eyes slitting devilishly. "I know I said I'd let you sleep after you fucked me dirty, Custis, but can we do one more thing? You can just lay back and relax."

She didn't wait for Longarm's reply. His dong, which

was slowly growing rigid once more, was apparently providing answer enough.

She lowered her head and nuzzled him back to full-blown life before slipping her succulent lips over his cock. She gave him a blow job—slowly, with excruciating purpose—to rival even those of the well-versed Cynthia Larimer. Wiping her mouth with the back of her hand, she snatched her rumpled nightdress off the floor, bid him adieu, and headed back to her own room via the balcony door.

The next morning, as Longarm, Tremaine, and Ranger Hall rode away from the Pleasant Valley headquarters after a hearty breakfast with Horace Woolyard, Longarm couldn't help feeling a sympathy pang for the ranch manager's daughter. Verna had slept in rather than join them for breakfast, but now Longarm could hear the faint tinkling of a piano in the house behind him.

It was a lonely, forlorn sound out here in the brassy morning light. Barely audible above the cicadas' buzz, the wind's rustle, and the incessant hammering arising from the blacksmith shop. Looking around at the endless expanse of scrub-covered hills, spotted here and there with white-faced cattle, Longarm could understand how a precocious, vibrant young woman could feel consumed by such a place.

And totally cut off from the larger world beyond.

Vibrant . . . Longarm winced at the rub of his McClellan saddle against his chafed member. Yes, the girl was definitely vibrant. So vibrant he'd had a hell of a time rolling himself out of bed at the first blush of dawn.

He glanced at Tremaine and Hall riding to his left along the chalky wagon trail, tufted here and there with Spanish bayonet. If either man was aware of Longarm's burning of the midnight oil with Woolyard's spry daughter, he didn't let on. The Scotchman's liquor had probably dropped both into a long, deep night's sleep, like the one Longarm himself should have had.

They stopped at midmorning to water their horses at a mortared stone trough fed by a spring bubbling from a low, rocky shelf. Smoking, they took some time to study the detailed map Woolyard had drawn of his range, with the locations of the other ranches residing inside the Pleasant Valley fence—as well the scene of the recent attack on him and his men—marked clearly in heavy black pencil.

"I say we start by trying to track the attackers to wherever in hell they came from. If their trail's too cold, then we start payin' visits to those other ranches—the ones on the state school land. We'll make Corpus's Wolf Creek outfit our first stop." Removing his cheroot from his teeth, Longarm glanced at the other men gathered around the large, butcher-paper map that Longarm had spread out atop a flat boulder. "Unless either of you boys has another plan?"

"Works fer me," said Hall. "But I got me a hunch whoever attacked Woolyard is long gone. Also got me a hunch it ain't one of the other ranchers out here, neither."

Tremaine was dampening his wadded neckerchief from his canteen. "Why's that?"

"Attacking the Pleasant Valley crew would only bring more trouble down on 'em. Shit, they're already gophers livin' right in the middle of a damn rattlesnake nest. True, a few of 'em might throw a rope over an unbranded Pleasant Valley calf once in a while. But running off with entire sections of herds?" Hall shook his head and raked a black hand through his short, curly black beard. "Nah. That'd just get 'em run out o' here on a long, greased rail."

"What about Corpus?" Longarm said. "Sounds like,

with all those hired guns he's got, he might have some high aspirations. Like maybe taking over this entire range for himself?"

"I've had me a change of heart about that old greaser. Shit, this range is too big for Corpus. He knows that. Those hired guns of his are for protection against Woolyard's curly wolves."

"Well, goddamnit, Eb!" Angrily, Tremaine sloshed more water onto his neckerchief and continued dabbing at his sunburned cheeks. "You think it's just cyclones swoopin' down and makin' all those cows disappear?"

"Cyclones? Nah," the Ranger said, turning and planting his gloved fists on his hips as he stared straight south. "I think it's Mescins up from the border."

Longarm and Tremaine both cast their gazes southward, into the brassy, hazy distance, toward Old Mexico. "That'd be a far piece to trail stolen cattle, through the Big Bend country and beyond. But, hell, I've known Mexicans to ride up into Colorado, swinging long loops over everything with horns they could find. Branded and unbranded."

"Well, shit," Tremaine said. "If we hadn't been ordered to stop our work out here and wait for one certain federal, we mighta had the mystery solved by now, and the rustlers behind bars." He knotted his neckerchief around his un- shaven neck and stomped back to his horse. "Way it is now, we're likely to be on this job till Christmas two years from now!"

"Better not take that long," Hall said. "Old Woolyard's given us ten days and not a wink later."

As the stock detective stepped into his saddle, Longarm glanced at Hall, who grinned, flashing his tobacco-stained teeth. "Don't mind him, Longarm. He's just jealous."

Longarm frowned. "Jealous of what?"

"Of that mattress dance you had last night with Miss Woolyard."

Longarm's jaw dropped to his chest. As Hall moseyed over to his own mount, grinning, very pleased with himself, Longarm said, "How in the hell—?"

Hall swung up into his saddle, the sun-dried leather creaking under his weight. "I never could pee indoors like civilized folk, so I hoofed it out to the privy last night, 'bout two o'clock or so. The shitter's on the backside of the house, don't ya know? I was just gettin' down to business when I heard what at first sounded like an Injun attack. Sure enough, I thought the Comanches were affectin' a night raid!"

He glanced at Longarm, who stood frozen and looking beleaguered.

"Then I seen a girl's silhouette through some third-story curtains, and I heard you give a whoop and a holler, like a wild old drover stompin' with his tail up on the Fourth of Joo-*ly*!"

With that, the black Ranger laughed and gigged his horse into an instant gallop after Tremaine, who rode, back straight in the saddle, down the rocky hill to the east. Hall tossed a knowing grin over his shoulder. "Tremaine—he's been tryin' to get in that girl's bloomers since she first came out here, and you had her screechin' for her momma after only a couple hours!"

The Ranger turned forward, threw his head back on his shoulders, and guffawed.

His own dust consumed him.

"Goddamnit," Longarm said as he climbed into his own saddle. "I don't remember her callin' for her momma." He heeled his horse after the other two riders, his brows beetled pensively.

He shook his head and chuckled. "Damn!"

# Chapter 9

Longarm squeezed the dried chunk of horse apple between his thumb and index finger. The fine grains of oat- and grass-flecked shit crumbled to dust and blew away on the hot wind.

The lawman stood and looked to the north, where jagged mounds of black rock humped before a vast tabletop mesa. He brushed his hand against his whipcord-clad thigh and loosened his shirt collar beneath the already-loose string tie that whipped back over his shoulder in the wind. Doffing his hat, he ran a hand through his sweaty, close-cropped hair, then reached for the canteen hanging from his saddle horn.

Though late in the year, it had to be close to ninety degrees out here.

Behind him, hoof thuds sounded, and, holding his canteen, he turned to see Tremaine and Hall loping toward him up a slight grade in the otherwise flat-bottomed desert bowl over which a few large, fluffy clouds floated. The clouds were as big as mountains, but out here, under all that arching sky, they appeared no larger than freight wagons.

This was the trio's second day on the trail out from the Pleasant Valley headquarters, and, like Longarm, the stock detective and the Ranger looked hot and dusty, as did their horses. The three men had separated several hours ago, to try to pick up the bushwhackers' trail, agreeing to meet here on the Trinidad flats at the edge of the lava bluffs at three o'clock. It was a little after three now, and as Longarm plucked the cork from his canteen and the two riders pulled their blowing horses up before him, he said, "Any luck, gents?"

"Couple horse tracks, spaced wide apart," Hall said, doffing his hat and running a sleeve of his sweat-soaked black shirt across his forehead. "Two, three days old. Mighta been Pleasant Valley cow nurses. Mighta been anybody."

Tremaine popped the cork on his own canteen. "I didn't come up with nothin' but a few grazing cows and a bobcat watchin' me from a post oak branch. Also found an old Comanche war lance." He patted the ancient, stone-tipped spear the hickory handle of which was badly splintered and weathered to a gunmetal gray, and which he'd strapped to the side of his saddle. "Gonna take it home and hang it over my fireplace. If I ever get home, that is."

He looked around at the large, sparse clouds and the sky, then shook his head and lifted it to drink from the hide-wrapped canteen.

"Well, they covered their tracks good—I'll give 'em that," Longarm said when he'd taken a drink of his own stale water. "But that horse apple there is about as old as the sign you cut, Hall. I'm gonna take a wild shot in the dark and say it's from them long-loopers that attacked Woolyard. Since we're out this far, we might as well follow whatever sign we cut, see where it leads."

"So, by which end should we grab the snake, amigo?" Hall asked. "That's big country in there. And snaggle-toothed as a dinosaur's mouth. We might go in there and never find our way out again, much less cattle rustlers."

"I agree," said Tremaine, tipping his head far back to dribble water over his sun-blistered cheeks. "Might be wise to just camp out here for a few days, see if them bush-whackers or rustlers or whoever they are show themselves again. I spied a good-sized herd o' cattle a couple miles southeast. They'd be easy pickin's for Hall's Mescins on their way back to Old Mexico."

"If it's Hall's Mescins we're after," Longarm said, loop-ing his canteen over his saddle horn and casting his gaze toward the dark, toothy lava bluffs once more. "And if they intend to head south anytime soon. Might be that *whoever* it is throwin' them mighty long loops is holin' up in a canyon in there somewheres, fattening a stolen herd of Pleasant Valley beef and passin' the time till Woolyard's fury over his aching ass dies down."

He narrowed a shrewd eye at his two partners. "Me, I think I'll head that way. If you boys want to wait here or, hell, even go on back to Claireville and wait for me with Sheriff Todd, that'd be fine as snake hair."

"Pshaw!" Hall scoffed. "And give you all the glory if you *do* find 'em?"

"Glory, hell!" intoned Tremaine, scrunching up his face at the black man. "I say if he wants to go in there and get himself greased by owlhoots or renegade Comanches, let him! I got me three silver cartwheels says if he sets off north, we'll never see him again, and neither will anyone else 'ceptin' the coyotes and buzzards up thataway!"

"You go on back to Claireville, then," Hall said. "Go on back and play two-handed stud with Ole Peg Leg himself.

Me, I'm ridin' north with Longarm, crazy as he obviously is. I got me a reputation to keep up."

"Ah, shit," Tremaine grumbled, hipping around in his saddle, a look of supreme frustration on his blond-stubbled face.

"You don't have to go." Longarm took his reins in one hand and stepped into his saddle, his mouth corners quirking in a cunning half smile. He'd wanted to ride alone at the start of the journey from Claireville, but that was before he'd gotten a firsthand look at how big this country was, at how vast the Pleasant Valley holdings were. If he was going to have any chance at all of running down the men who'd bushwhacked Woolyard, he'd need every pair of eyes at his disposal.

"Nah," he added, knowingly overplaying his hand. "Go on back to town and wait for us there. I'm sure Sheriff Todd would 'preciate the company." He winked at Hall, who chuckled and gave his head a quick shake.

Tremaine squinted one eye at Hall. He squinted the other eye at Longarm. Then he gave a caustic chuff and settled himself in his saddle. "All right. I'm in, goddamnit."

"Now that that's settled," Longarm said, heeling the big roan into a slow walk down the north side of the scrubby hill, "I suggest we spread out again. Best chance of us overtaking the bushwhackers' main trail. Any point in them rocks yonder that might make a good place for us all to deadhead for, meet up maybe tomorrow or the next day?"

Judging by the apparent vastness of the rocky country ahead, fronting the mesa that looked as large as all of the area taken up by the growing city of Denver, they'd need at least two days to even start covering it.

"Armadillo Rock," Hall said. "You'll see it. Looks just like its name. It's hunkered down on the east side of that mesa yonder. That's Comanche Hill, though there's nothin' hilly about it." He hipped around in his saddle to glance at Tremaine flanking him and Longarm sort of lounging in his saddle while he built a quirley with his gloved hands. "I ain't never been that far. You, Hank?"

"I been out there with half a dozen cavalry back in the day, chasin' Comanche. Wouldn't wanna be out there with just three. Shit, there's still Comanche out that way, and probably a good number of desperadoes up from Mexico. They den up out there, don't ya know? Those men could be dry as a dusty rain barrel at the end of August, and they'd still just as soon potshoot you from a hundred yards away as ask you for a drink of water."

"That's good to know," Longarm grunted, swerving his horse to the left and heeling it into a lope. "Keep a finger on your trigger, fellas. And one eye on your backtrail!"

A couple of hundred yards later he slowed the stallion atop a knoll and glanced to his right to see the Ranger and the stock detective branching off on their own unseen trails. Hall headed straight north while Tremaine angled north and east. Their horses lifted small puffs of brown dust over the buck brush and the broad, flat spines of the agave plants behind them.

It didn't take long for both men to shrink to the size of polka dots on a faraway neckerchief, and to disappear behind buttes and mesquite-sheathed draws.

Longarm adjusted his .44 on his left hip, angling the grip toward his belly where he could quickly grab it if he needed to, and heeled the roan down the slope toward the shoulder of tall sandstone pedestal rock. The formation appeared to be only a few hundred yards away, shimmering in the liquid heat hovering just above the horizon, but Longarm didn't reach the rock until almost sundown.

In fact, he stopped at the base of the rock, as it would soon be too dark to push any farther into the lava bluffs without risking injury to his horse and thus himself. He tended the roan, built a small cook fire, and settled in for the night.

Coyotes howled and yipped so close to his camp that he kept waking up, reaching for his gun, and imagining Comanche warriors bounding toward his bedroll, all armed with spears like the one Tremaine had found. Later, when the coyotes had drifted off to a different wash, he dreamt he was watching Verna Woolyard play the piano on a barren West Texas hilltop clad in nothing except a single hawk feather like those worn by fair Comanche maidens.

Otherwise, she was as naked as she'd been night before last, when he was ramrodding her doggie style.

By that time, dawn was a pale flush in the eastern sky, and Longarm pried himself up out of the hole for his hip that he'd kicked out of the dirt and sand with his boot, and started a breakfast fire with dry bunch grass and mesquite shavings. He gave the roan a quick rubdown and hoof inspection in spite of having done both the night before, for out here a healthy mount was worth its weight in gold. As he inspected a front hock and cannon for scrapes and bruises, the horse tried to nip the back of Longarm's neck. The lawman felt the warm breath above his collar and, cursing, twisted away.

"Oh, no you don't."

The horse snorted and rolled its eyes friskily, self-satisfied.

Obviously, the big stallion was feeling just fine.

Longarm threw the leather to it, stowed his cooking utensils in his war bag, and mounted up, to continue his meandering northward course around bluffs and hills and the giant knife slashes of dry washes. In the early afternoon he was deep in the lava bluffs, with large upthrusts of black volcanic rock all around him—dinosaur spines and camel-backs of weathered minerals hiccupped by the Earth over eons and down across the ages.

He was on a steep, gravelly bluff shoulder, weaving among sandstone boulders, when, in the corner of his right eye, he saw a shadow move across the face of the rock beside him. He turned quickly to his left. A man dropped toward him from a jagged-edged boulder—a swarthy fellow with long black hair and distinctly Indian features beneath the brim of a palm-leaf sombrero. Longarm saw the man's coffee-brown eyes glint devilishly and a knife in the man's right fist wink with menace.

And then the man was on him, a good two hundred pounds of sweating gristle and muscle punching him off his right stirrup fender. He hit the ground on his back. The air was hammered from his lungs with a loud *whuff.*

The Indian's lips stretched back from his teeth, and his eyes narrowed to slits. "*Ayeeee!*"

Longarm thought the cry was a victory yell. But then he saw that the knife, instead of having been driven hilt-deep in his chest, was still firmly gripped by the swarthy gent's fist. And that the man's wrist was locked tight in Longarm's own hand.

Automatically, Longarm must have grabbed it when the Indian had slammed into him.

Still, the Indian had the upper hand, as it were. Grunting and groaning and spitting, he clambered onto his knees and drove the knife down, down toward Longarm's sharply corded neck. Longarm was dazed from his impact with the ground, birds chirping in his ears and fire balloons bursting behind his eyes.

Somehow, he kept his left hand wrapped around the Indian's right wrist. He was vaguely surprised that the blade was not moving more quickly to his throat, and that his carotid artery was still intact. Amazing how much strength a man could summon, despite his overall physical state, when his life was hanging by a weathered whang string over the yawning pits of coal-black eternity.

As the Indian kicked and squirmed, driving the knife to within four then two inches of Longarm's bulging neck muscles, Longarm got his other hand up and laid it flat across the Indian's hawk-nosed, hairless face. The man groaned and cursed in Spanish as Longarm drove his fingertips into the Indian's eyes. Involuntarily, the attacker closed his eyes, and at the same time, suddenly more focused on the health of his vision than on the kill, he slightly relaxed the arm driving the knife.

Longarm's fingers pushed the man's eyes a good inch into his skull. The Indian screamed and kicked like a stuck pig. Longarm drew his right hand back suddenly, clenched his fist, and rammed it forward. He didn't have much room for a windup, but his knuckles smacked the man's cheek with enough force that the Indian flew with a savage cry to Longarm's left.

The knife hit the ground with a clink.

Blinking, Longarm heaved himself to his knees. He was trying to gain his feet, but his buzzing ears and aching head made his body feel heavy and weak. The Indian acquired his own feet first, batwing chaps flapping against his dusty canvas breeches and the tops of his stockmen's boots. His spurs trilled. Just as Longarm shoved off a knee and had started turning to face the man, the Indian bolted toward him, crouching.

The Indian caught him with his head and shoulder buried in Longarm's belly. Again, Longarm hit the ground on his back. Again, the air left his lungs with a loud grunt, though not quite as loud as last time.

Then he and the Indian were rolling down a steep, gravelly hill toward a canyon yawning a good distance below. The Indian rolled over Longarm. Longarm rolled over the Indian. Both men were trying to stop their fall while at the same time flailing out at each other with their feet and fists.

Their bodies separated, and Longarm twisted around so that his boots faced downhill. He saw a spindly shrub to his left and grabbed it. The branches cracked, and thorns dug into his flesh, but the hold stopped his descent. Looking across his chest, he saw the Indian, hair and chaps flying, as the man piled up against a low boulder a few feet farther down the steep grade.

Rocks and dust tumbled down the upslope. The Indian's spurs smacked the rock with a loud, grating *ching*.

Again, after only a quick shake of his head and a blink or two of his bloodshot eyes, the Indian was back on his feet. As Longarm got his own feet under him, his attacker reached for a big, ivory-handled horse pistol holstered for the cross-draw on his right hip, opposite from where a large, beaded knife sheath hung empty.

Longarm might have been slower on his feet, but his own Colt .44 was in his hand in a wink. He hoped that his own aimed pistol would forestall the Indian, but when the man ratcheted the horse pistol's hammer back, eyes glinting darkly, Longarm fired.

His bullet took the man through his belly, causing dust to puff from his red-and-black cotton shirt and punching him back on his heels. As he stumbled backward, spurs gouging the rocks and sand, he fired his big Colt into the ground in front of his boots.

"*Mierda!*" he grunted as a spur clipped a tuft of Spanish bayonet.

He dropped his hands, threw his arms out, and hit the ground on his butt. The grade was steeper here, dropping sharply to the canyon below. The man tried to stay his fall, but, reaching out, he grabbed a prickly pear plant. Screaming, he released the plant and fell backward, rolling wildly, arms and legs flying, spurs lifting a raucous rhythm and throwing up sand and small rocks.

Just above the lip of the canyon, the grade's pitch became less sharp. Somehow, just as the man's knees dropped into the canyon, with the rocky chasm yawning a good sixty or seventy feet beneath him, the Indian got himself stopped.

He clung to a knob of rock with one hand. He stared up the slope at Longarm, his jaws hard, teeth gritted, black eyes desperate and beseeching.

Staring down the slope, Longarm depressed the Colt's hammer. He slipped the gun into its holster and began side-stepping down the grade. Several times he slipped and dropped to a knee, but he hurried. The knuckles of the Indian's hand that clung to the small knob of rock were growing whiter and whiter, and the man was gritting his teeth so desperately that Longarm thought he could hear a couple crack.

Finally, Longarm was ten feet from the canyon. He dropped to a knee, turning so that he was facing parallel to the canyon lip, then reached for the Indian's hand. His own hand was within a few inches of the Indian's before the man's mouth opened, his eyes widened, and his white-knuckled hand slipped off the rock.

The man's black eyes grazed Longarm's just before they dropped below the canyon's lip, and disappeared. There was an echoing yell, shrill with horror. There was a soft smacking sound, barely audible above the diminishing echoes rolling up from below.

Silence.

"Shit!"

Longarm rose from his knee, carefully planted his boots at the edge of the canyon, and peered down. The Indian lay on the white rocks between two boulders below, on his side, one knee bent. His hair made a black halo around his head.

The rocks around his head and his hair were painted red.

# Chapter 10

Longarm would have liked to know who the Indian had been and why he'd welcomed Longarm to the caprock canyon country with a rusty, razor-edged pigsticker. He also would have liked to know why the man had tried to take him to the dance with a knife when he could have potshot him much more easily, and probably lived to tell the tale.

Scouting around, looking for other possible bushwhackers, Longarm found a canteen and a well-tended Spencer repeating rifle near the perch from which the knife-wielding Indian had propelled himself.

Maybe the man had just been bored and wanted a challenge. Or maybe he'd been wondering who Longarm was, and why he was here, and he couldn't have gotten that out of a corpse. Could be the man, who'd obviously boasted some Apache or Comanche blood, had wanted a little entertainment by way of learning how loud and how long he could get the white man to scream.

Longarm didn't think so. His attacker may have been Indian, but he was no bronco Apache. More likely, he was one of the very rustlers Longarm was looking for, and had been stationed here to watch the trail. A sentinel.

If so, Longarm might well be getting close to the rustler's lair.

Whatever the truth, the Indian had taken it with him to the blood-washed rocks on the canyon floor. So, uneasily, keeping his rifle ready in his right hand, with a cartridge seated in the firing breech and the hammer set to off-cock, Longarm ran down his horse, stepped into the McClellan saddle, and continued up the trail. As he rode, he raked his gaze from one side of the trail to the other, his keen, experienced eyes probing every nook and cranny in the black mounds of ancient lava spiked here and there with broad-leafed pear cactus and cat's claw.

Slowly, warily, he rode through the deep-cut, rugged country, under a liquid, hammering sun. He came upon the intermittent tracks of a single rider and a couple of relatively fresh piles of horse shit, and his heartbeat quickened slightly. Riding with the butt of his Winchester snugged tight against his thigh, holding the roan's reins in his left hand up close to his chest, he continued northward.

Several hours after his dustup with the Indian, he drew rein in a broad, deep, rock-strewn wash. A chill ran up and down his backbone. Gooseflesh rose like that lifted by a sudden prairie wind on the northern plains.

But he was far from Dakota country. The temperature had to be close to ninety out here, and not a cloud in the brassy sky.

Longarm held the roan's reins taught in his left fist. He caressed the Winchester's hammer with his right thumb and swiveled his head around slowly, sliding his gaze along the rock- and brush-strewn rim of the wash on both sides of him. Behind, the wash disappeared, tunnel-like, through overarching shrubs. Ahead, the gap was a little wider, its eroded banks webbed with old roots and gravel and what looked like bits of animal bone.

The wash appeared to fork about fifty yards farther on, but Longarm couldn't tell for sure from this vantage.

What he did know was that warning bells were tolling in his ears, which still hadn't quite stopped ringing after the pummeling he'd taken from the knife-wielding red man. Over the years he'd learned not to ignore his instincts. Somewhere around here, ahead or behind or up one of the banks, trouble lurked. Sure as the sun angled off to his left in the vast Texas sky.

He took another good, long look around, then continued slowly forward, the shrubs pulling slightly back on both sides of him. The McClellan's drying leather squeaked softly. The roan's shod hooves clacked off the water-polished stones. Occasionally a quail cooed or a desert thrush piped. The sun beat down—a physical heat that lay heavy on the testy lawman's shoulders and against his left cheek.

Trouble would come from that direction, he figured. Left. A bushwhacker would take advantage of the light behind him—in Longarm's eyes.

There was, indeed, a fork in the wash. Longarm drew rein in the middle of the fork and looked around. A clatter rose to his right, and he turned his head sharply to see a stone rolling down the steep, chalky bank.

"Ah, amigo, welcome to Dead Man Wash!"

Longarm's heart thudded as he jerked his head back to see two men standing atop the high bank around which the trail forked. He hadn't seen them before. It was as though they'd materialized out of thin air—a stocky gent with long, blond hair falling straight down from a broad-brimmed leather hat, and the stock detective, Hank Tremaine.

The blond gent, who had a deeply seamed and sunburned face, wore ratty cowboy garb, including chaps and undershot stockmen's boots. He was holding an oiled Smith & Wesson against the stock detective's dimpled right jaw hinge. He was grinning, green eyes sparking with shrewd cunning.

Tremaine's hat was gone. His sandy hair was mussed. Both of his holsters were empty. Both eyes were swollen nearly closed, and his shirt hung off his shoulders in blood-stained strips. He'd been beaten and whipped. His knees were bent, shaking weakly. Both hands were behind him, probably tied. The stocky man held him by one arm and jabbed the Smithy hard against Tremaine's cheek.

The stock detective groaned and tipped his battered head back slightly.

The blond man spoke with a Mexican accent—a gringo raised south of the Border. "Señor, disarm yourself, *por favor*, and step down from your saddle. Otherwise, sorry to say, I will blow this gringo's head off his shoulders." One half of his mouth curled. "He is your partner, I take it, no?"

Longarm's eyes shuttled around the bank before him. They picked out a rifle barrel aimed toward him from just behind Tremaine and to his right. The man aiming the rifle was mostly concealed by a mesquite shrub. Longarm could see only a sharp chin and an unshaven jaw, the chin thong of a hat dangling toward the Spencer's cocked hammer.

Longarm looked at the blond Mexican. "Him?" He chuffed. "Don't know him from Adam."

Tremaine smiled slightly, then winced as a pain spasm nipped him.

"No, amigo?" The blond gent feigned surprise, ignoring the fly buzzing about his thin-lipped mouth and his straggly mustache that was bleached nearly white. "Then you don't mind if I blow his jaw off his face, uh?"

The blond gent ground his teeth and rolled his eyes toward Tremaine. His trigger finger tightened slightly.

"Hold on," Longarm growled.

"No," croaked Tremaine, shaking his head. "He'll kill me anyway, Longarm. Then he'll kill you."

The blond hard case said, "Longarm? I like that name. Longarm! You have one arm longer than the other, amigo? My brother was like that, but he was ugly, too—not handsome like me—so we called him *Perro*. Dawg!" He chuckled for a time, and then his eyes narrowed once more. "Now, *por favor*. Disarm yourself and step down from your saddle. Your friend has been very uncooperative. Of course, Miguel and I only just started *encouraging* him. But it is necessary for us to know how many of you are out here, sniffing around like desert lobos."

"They got a herd," Tremaine said thickly, his swollen eyes regarding Longarm sharply. "In a box canyon. All Pleasant Valley Bar-V brands."

"Amigo," the blond Mex said, ignoring the stock detective and nodding at the rifle in Longarm's hands. "You can die now, with your friend, or later. It is your choice. Me, I would always choose later."

Again, Longarm heard the clatter of a dislodged stone behind him. He'd just rolled his eyes in that direction, when a rifle cracked. There was a *thwack*, then the blond Mex gave a grunt. He jerked back, a neat round hole in the middle of his red-tan forehead, his lower jaw falling slack.

The pistol in his hand barked, but the rifle bullet had nudged the Smithy away from Tremaine's face, and the Smithy's round barked off a rock in the wash's right fork, some yards ahead of Longarm.

Holding tight to the prancing roan's reins, Longarm looked to his right. Atop the bank, among the dry shrubs,

Ranger Ebenezer Hall knelt on one knee, powder smoke wafting around his mahogany features as he quickly levered a fresh shell into his Henry's breech. Before Longarm had turned from the man, the Ranger had fired the Henry a second time.

When Longarm looked back toward Tremaine, he saw the man aiming the rifle from down low in the brush, the face of the second rustler lifting sharply. Longarm triggered his own rifle, and smoke puffed among the olive foliage around him. The bullet drilled the bank of the wash just beneath Hall, who lowered his Henry to shout, "Do believe we wore out our welcome, gents! Let's light a shuck on outta here!"

At the same time, shouts rose from the bank behind Tremaine, as did the thud of galloping horses. Longarm couldn't see the riders, but riders they were, and they were approaching at a fast clip.

He heeled the roan toward the bank straight ahead, where, after the blond Mex had fallen in the brush, Tremaine had dropped to his knees and was now down on all fours, head hanging down beneath his shoulders. He was damn near unconscious.

"Come on, Hank!" Longarm shouted, putting the roan close to the bank and throwing an arm up toward the battered stock detective. "Company comin'. Let's vamoose!"

A rifle barked in the brush behind Tremaine. Then another. Hall cursed and fired three quick rounds, evoking more shouting from the oncoming riders, whom Longarm still couldn't see from his position at the bottom of the wash.

"Comin'," Tremaine groaned, trying to push himself to his feet but having little success beyond bobbing his head. "I'm comin', goddamnit. D-don't rush me."

"Goddamnit!" Longarm turned to Hall. "Keep covering us!"

"That's what I'm tryin' to do, but there's a shitload of nasty-lookin' hombres headed this way, and there's more coming from up above!"

As the Henry leaped and roared in Hall's hands, Longarm jumped out of his saddle and hastily threw his reins over a shrub growing out of the bank before him. The ten-foot bank was steep, so instead of trying to climb it, he jumped straight up, grabbed the brushy lip, and hoisted himself up and over the top.

Tremaine was crawling toward him, moving slowly and wincing and groaning with every move.

Longarm dropped beside the man. "Can you stand?"

"What you think I'm tryin' to do—pretend I'm a fuckin' turtle?"

Behind Longarm, a horse whinnied loudly. Hooves thundered and brush snapped. A pistol barked, and Longarm flinched as the bullet sizzled just over his head. Turning, he palmed his Colt and fired three quick shots as two riders materialized from the dusty, olive brush.

One rider screamed and sank sideways. The horse of the second man bucked suddenly, and the man grunted as he rolled backward out of his saddle. Across the wash, Hall was firing with his sixteen-shot Henry. Longarm figured the Ranger had about five or six shots left before he'd need to reload.

"Come on!" Longarm crouched under Tremaine's left arm, heaved the man to his feet, and half-carried, half-dragged him to the lip of the bank.

He held Tremaine's arm as he shoved the man over the side. Tremaine dropped straight down, boots skidding along the side of the bank. When his feet were near the bottom,

Longarm released his hand, and as Tremaine fell hard to both knees, Longarm threw his arms out and leaped. He hit the wash's rocky floor on both feet, bending his knees to absorb the impact.

Gritting his teeth against the aggravated pounding in his ears, he grabbed Tremaine and wrestled the man onto the roan's back, behind the McClellan saddle.

As he started to grab his reins from the shrub, another rider pounded into the small clearing atop the bank in front of him, with two more flanking the first. Hall drilled one with his Henry, but the first rider, a gangly, hawk-faced gent with flat, arrogant eyes under the brim of his low-crowned cream hat, extended a rifle toward Longarm.

The man's horse pitched at the same time the Winchester in his hands roared. The slug screeched off a rock to Longarm's right, causing the roan to scream and buck-kick, nearly unseating Tremaine, who threw himself forward over the saddle.

Longarm had his .44 out of its holster in an instant and emptied its cylinder into the chest of the hawk-faced gent. The man stretched his lips back from his teeth, threw his Winchester over his head, and, sagging atop his pitching dun stallion, disappeared back behind the edge of the bank.

The skitter-hopping roan had jerked its reins free of the shrub, and Longarm, hearing more riders closing on him fast, had to run the reins down and step on them before he could grab them and, holstering his empty Colt, swing into the hurricane deck in front of Tremaine.

Slugs screamed around him and hammered the rocks as he heeled the roan into an instant gallop toward the east side of the draw, Hall yelling above his roaring Henry, "*Shit*! This don't look good, fellers. This don't look good *a'tall*!"

# Chapter 11

Hall disappeared as Longarm and Tremaine lunged toward the far side of the wash atop the nickering roan. As Longarm turned the frightened horse down yet another right fork in the wash, he saw Hall leap from the bank ahead and into the saddle of his steeldust waiting below.

Sliding his empty Henry into its scabbard, the Ranger glanced over his shoulder at Longarm and Tremaine, whose head rested against Longarm's back. The black Ranger's dark eyes were white-ringed as they probed the forking wash behind Longarm.

Longarm shot past him as Hall gave a raucous bellow and gouged his spurs into the steeldust's flanks.

The roan being weighed down by two riders, Hall caught up to Longarm and Tremaine in no time, and soon both horses were plunging abreast down the broadening wash. Longarm could feel Tremaine sagging behind him, shifting loosely back there atop Longarm's rain-slicker–wrapped bedroll, and the lawman hoped the man was conscious enough to hold on.

Random gunfire, shouts, and the thuds of hammering

hooves hadn't ceased since Longarm had maneuvered Tremaine off the bank, and they continued now behind the three fleeing riders. Slugs sliced the air around them, screeching past and hammering rocks with billowing dust puffs and whining ricochets.

Longarm spared a quick glance behind.

Dust broiled back there in the ever-widening wash, and he could make out three or four front riders clad in sombreros and crisscrossed bandoliers, with dusters or canvas jackets whipping in the wind. The pursuers were pushing up out of that broiling brown cloud as though their horses were propelled by it.

Rifles and pistols flashed. The reports echoed loudly, off the walls of the wash, shuddering like hammered steel cables.

Behind Longarm, Tremaine sagged. Beneath him, the roan blew, fagged. It had been a hard ride for the horse, through sparsely watered country, even before they'd come upon the man trap. Now, with two riders, it was even tougher.

Longarm glanced at Hall riding low in his saddle to Longarm's right, the Ranger's weathered hat basted by the wind against his forehead. "We're gonna have to fort up!"

Hall nodded and cast another look behind. As he did so, a hole suddenly appeared in the front of his hat brim. He rolled his eyes up to give it skeptical consideration, then hunkered lower and raised his elbows as he and Longarm continued more or less east along the gently snaking, ever rising and leveling wash.

As the wash's banks dropped and fell away, Longarm found himself climbing a long, low, boulder-strewn hill toward a summit about a mile straight ahead. All around— near and far—were stone dikes, rocky shelves, escarpments, and more black mounds of ancient volcanoes and lava rubble.

The sun was angling behind him, the light softening, and shadows were bleeding out from every rock and shrub.

Their pursuers, apparently mounted on fresher horses than their quarry, were gaining on Longarm and his two partners. The bullets were slicing the air ever closer to Longarm and the lunging roan, and several times he had felt the horse flinch at a graze.

"Up there!" Hall shouted, looking toward a dinosaur spine of black rock humping up a hundred yards ahead and left.

Just as Longarm began to angle toward the formation, Hall's horse screamed. It dropped as though the ground had suddenly been pulled out from under it.

Hall yelled, and then he and the horse fell behind Longarm in a churning dust cloud from which came the raucous thuds of tumbling man and animal and the tooth-gnashing snaps of breaking bones.

"Ah, Christ!" Tremaine exclaimed thickly in Longarm's right ear.

Longarm jerked back on his own reins, and as the roan slowed, he turned it sideways to look back in horror at the steeldust that lay with its head facing the way they'd come. Covered with a good two inches of black dust and gravel, the horse wasn't moving.

Hall lay in a heap ahead of it, and he wasn't moving, either. But just as Longarm began to urge the roan back toward the fallen Ranger, Hall heaved himself to his knees. He spat dust and grit from his lips and brushed a hand against the grip of his holstered revolver, making sure it was still there on his hip.

Longarm glanced at their pursuers charging up the grade

behind them, four men out front riding abreast and yipping like lobos on the blood trail. "You all right?"

Hall muttered something that Longarm couldn't quite make out above the yipping and hoof clomping and gunfire behind the Ranger, but it sounded like "Shit."

A bullet blew up dust to Hall's right. It snapped him to full attention, and, his hat hanging down his back by its chin thong, he swung his head toward the approaching horde.

"Shit!" he shouted.

On hands and knees he scrambled back toward the steeldust.

Longarm quickly raised his Winchester and snapped off two quick shots to slow the oncoming gun wolves. He shouted to Hall, "This way, fool!"

"I gotta get my Henry!"

Longarm glanced uptrail. There was a low shelf about thirty yards away, the highest point attainable now that Hall was on foot. As a bullet kissed his neck like the smooch of a sharp-toothed whore, making him grit his teeth, Longarm batted his heels against the roan's flanks and yelled, "*Ha-yah!*"

The roan didn't so much lunge as lean forward and shamble up to the shelf on wobbly knees. When Longarm had stopped the horse down the far side of the rocky bench, out of sight for the moment from the gun wolves charging up his backtrail, he swung his right boot over the roan's neck and dropped straight down to the ground.

There was no time to help Tremaine down. Hall was in dire need of covering fire. Sharply levering a fresh shell into the Winchester's breech, Longarm bolted back up to the rocky ledge, dropped down behind it, and fired two quick shots, blowing one gun wolf out of his saddle and causing another to jerk back sharply on his claybank's

reins, bringing the mount to a skidding, screaming halt
about fifty yards down the long, boulder-strewn slope.

Hall had grabbed his Henry, his canteen, and his saddlebags, and was covering the thirty yards between his dead
horse and Longarm at a crouching, knock-kneed run. He
was holding his left arm down close to his side, as though
he'd been pinked there, or had injured the wing in the vio-
lent fall.

"Hurry!" Longarm yelled, then triggered two more
shots, evoking a yelp from one of the pursuers and causing
the entire wave of men and horses now to hesitate.

"What you think I'm doin'?" Hall said, breathless, as he
approached the top of the rocky shelf. "Stoppin' to brew
bellywash?"

As the hard cases yelled and continued to trigger shots
up toward the bench but not with as much piss and vinegar
as before, Longarm stood, grabbed Hall's right arm, and
pulled the Ranger down behind the covering rocks. Farther
down that side of the crest, Tremaine had managed to dis-
mount the roan by himself and was slouching back up toward the peak.

His face looked as though he'd been stung by a hundred
enraged hornets. His sweaty, sandy hair slid around in the
dry wind.

"One of you gents got a gun for me?" he said as he
dropped heavily to his knees behind Longarm and Hall. He
chuffed without mirth. "I sorta had mine confiscated by
them ringtails."

A bullet slammed into a rock in front of Hall. The black
Ranger flinched as he glanced at Tremaine. "Hell, you can't
shoot. You can't *see* to shoot! They done walloped you
good."

As Longarm thumbed fresh shells into his cartridge belt

and edged a look down the grade from between two rocks, Tremaine said, "I can see just fine."

"What'd you do, Hank?" Hall asked as he triggered a shot at the gun wolves, whose own shooting had slowed, probably while they scrambled for their own cover. "You waltz right into them rustlers' lair?"

"I reckon that's what I did all right. Suddenly, I had three men all around me, aimin' rifles from big, black rocks."

"Here," Longarm said as he extended his Colt butt first to the stock detective. "You see any cattle?"

Tremaine took the gun and spun the cylinder, hefting the .44's weight in his hand.

"No, but I sure seen their sign. Smelled 'em and heard 'em, too. They got 'em a sizable herd in a box canyon. I do believe Hall had it right. They're Mescins come up to rob Pleasant Valley blind."

Hall aimed down his Henry's barrel. Not finding a target, he withdrew the rifle and ran a hand through his dust-caked, curly black hair. "Probably herd the cows across the Rio Grande, alter the brands, and sell back in Texas again as Mexican-raised beef. El Paso or San Antonio, most likely."

Tremaine hunkered down low and peered through a gap in the low wall of cracked boulders that had pushed up from the top of the hill a hundred or so million years ago. He snaked the Colt through the crack, stuck his tongue out as he aimed, and fired.

"Damn," he said, "they're forted up good."

Longarm was hunkered to the left of the other two men, snaking his Winchester between two boulders. He'd discovered a man in buckskins and wearing a large, brown felt hat moving at a stealthy crouch amid rocks and cedars down the slope and left, nearly hidden by a shallow draw.

The man disappeared behind a cracked, black boulder with an agave growing in the middle of it. He reappeared a moment later, crouched over his rifle as he worked his way around the side of the hill, likely trying to flank Longarm, Hall, and Tremaine.

Longarm drew a bead on him and squeezed the Winchester's trigger. The rifle roared. The man in the brown hat twisted around, stumbled sideways, and disappeared. Dust rose where he'd fallen.

One of the other pursuers shouted something Longarm couldn't hear from this distance.

"Damn!" Hall exclaimed. "You pinked him right good. Didn't know you federals came with sharpshootin' credentials."

"We don't," Longarm said, withdrawing the Winchester from the gap between the rocks. The spent brass jacket arced over his shoulder as he snapped the breech open, then seated a fresh round in the chamber. "That was a desperation shot. We got one blown horse amongst the three of us, so we best make each shot count, gents. If'n we wanna make it outta here, that is."

Hall sighed. "I hear that." He squinted an eye at Longarm. "You get a sense of how many's down there?"

"Ten. Maybe more."

Tremaine dabbed at a cut above his eye with his wadded neckerchief. "There's more than that in the whole group, because I seen several more in the cliffs on the other side of the box canyon they're holding the beeves in, and I seen their remuda. I'd say there's at least fifteen men in this whole operation. Might be closer to twenty."

Hall was aiming again, making a sour, frustrated expression as sweat dug troughs through the dust on his cheeks. "Yeah, they prob'ly left a few with the herd."

Longarm was on an elbow, keeping his head below the low rocks, looking around, his mind working slowly, methodically, trying to figure a way out of another tight spot.

Tremaine must have read his mind. "They get around behind us, we're finished."

Longarm continued looking around. To either side and behind, there was nothing but open country. No good cover that the ambushers might use to flank Longarm's party. Of course, they could get around them after dark, but the sky was clear. Likely, it would be a clear, quiet night, and their footsteps, no matter how quietly they tried to move, would give them away.

He stole another look between the two boulders in front of him, scrutinizing the rock-strewn slope. There was a broad, relatively open area, stippled with only small stones, cactus, and clumps of dry, colorless brush, directly below the rocky bench behind which Longarm and the other two men had taken cover. Anyone trying to traverse that open ground would be an easy target for a pistol, even easier for a repeating rifle.

As long as Longarm and his partners could hold the bench, they'd be all right. But they couldn't hold it forever, as they had only so much ammunition and water.

Hall snapped off a shot down the grade. His slug barked off a boulder. A man cursed wickedly, as though he might have gotten a finger blown off. Hall snorted dryly as he ejected his spent cartridge casing, seated fresh, and glanced at Longarm.

"You thinking what I'm thinking?"

"What's that?"

"That we're in shit soup up to our eyebrows."

Longarm glanced around and scratched his cheek with his middle finger. "It's a tight hand."

"Sorry, fellers," Tremaine said. "I'm the fool that got us into this. Why don't you both take the roan? I'll stay here and keep 'em busy until you're clear."

"Don't be a fool," Longarm said. "Any one of us could have ridden into that trap in this canker-on-the-devil's-ass country."

Tremaine chuckled. "Thanks for sayin' so."

"Ain't just sayin' it. Besides, that roan isn't carrying even one rider till it's had some time to rest."

"You got another way?" Tremaine wanted to know.

Hall sighed as he stared down the hill. "Maybe if we can hold 'em off long enough, they'll get bored and wander away."

Neither Longarm nor Tremaine said anything.

"Yeah, maybe not," Hall said wryly. "Maybe they'll just keep us pinned down up here till we're outta ammunition. Then they'll finish us. Coyote bait."

There was a sudden scurry of movement from below. Both Longarm and Hall poked their rifles into the gaps between the boulders in front of them.

"Hold up," Tremaine grunted. He was down on one elbow and hip, staring through a V-notch on the other side of Hall, to Longarm's right. "They're just tryin' to draw our fire."

Longarm cursed under his breath as he continued staring down the hill, catching occasional, fleeting glimpses of the gunhands below, holed up behind boulders, rocks, and hummocks. A couple were hunkered low in a cow wallow, only the tip of a rifle barrel and the feather adorning a hat showing above the wallow's lip.

Longarm squinted at the west-falling sun. "Only about an hour of light left. After dark we might be able to scramble on outta here."

Even as he voiced the idea, he doubted it would work. It was all open country behind them, to the southeast. The gunnies would easily run them down.

"Well," he said, turning to the roan that stood hang-headed twenty yards down the grade from the bench. "The roan's our hole card. One of us'll ride it out of here after dark, try to locate a couple more horses, and bring 'em back before dawn."

Hall nodded as he stared thoughtfully at the weary roan. "Might work. The Corpus ranch is about ten, twelve miles southeast. If old man Corpus himself ain't in with this bunch, he's liable to lend us a couple mounts. Of course, the chances of getting back here in time to save the two of us who stay . . ."

The Ranger let his voice trail off, as there was no point in finishing the thought. The danger was obvious. It was a perilous, likely deadly, situation.

Longarm turned to Tremaine. "Hank, you'll go. You can't shoot for shit with those swollen eyes anyway."

Tremaine shook his head slowly, wearily. "I'll never make it. I think them bastards dislocated my shoulder. Right now I'm ready to curl up and pass out. I'll be even less use later on."

To Hall, Longarm said, "All right—you'll go."

"We'll flip for it."

"Shit, it ain't like whoever rides out of here is in the clear. They might hear the horse and ride it down, and there's damn little cover out thataway."

"Just the same, let's flip for it. Whoever calls it right goes." Hall pulled a silver piece out of his trouser pocket. "Call it."

As Hall flipped the coin, Longarm called heads.

It was heads.

"All right, then," Longarm sighed. He glanced at the roan, then crawled down the slope away from the bench. "I reckon I better unsaddle him, see if I can pump some life back into him."

# Chapter 12

From ahead and along the left side of the narrow, night-cloaked wash, a wooden snap sounded. There was a whiny rasp. Instantly, Longarm jerked the roan to a stop. His Colt was in his right hand, the pistol cocked and aimed straight out from his hip.

He squeezed the pistol's grip as a low, dark figure pushed out from the brush on the left side of the wash, about a hundred feet ahead. The figure stole into the wash, moving slick as smoke toward Longarm.

The dark form stopped suddenly. Two copper lights shone in the darkness of the wash, beneath a sky in which the moon sailed behind high, thin clouds like gauzy curtains over a lit window. The twin lights flickered simultaneously. Vagrant moonlight slithered like quicksilver through spindly branches along the wash and touched the coyote's gray-dun fur. As the animal lifted its head, the light limned its sharp snout.

Giving a low whimper, the coyote turned, shambled with its head and tail low, and disappeared into the brush on the opposite side of the wash. There was the slight clink of a stone, then silence.

Before Longarm was only the tunnel-like wash under the moonlit sky, with here and there a distant formation silhouetted against the violet horizon. Longarm depressed the Colt's hammer, the click sounding inordinately loud in the still, silent night, and slipped the pistol back into its holster. Carefully, purposefully, he flipped the keeper thong over the hammer and snapped it home.

He would take no chance with the .44. Aside from the double-barreled derringer in his vest pocket, the .44 was the only weapon he had. He'd left his rifle with Hall and Tremaine, along with all his spare shells excepting the six in the Colt's cylinder and six more in his cartridge belt. The Ranger and the stock detective, alone on the high plateau behind the low, rocky spine, and with a dozen or so cutthroats pinning them down, would likely need the ammunition more than Longarm would.

If Longarm found that he did need it, no amount was likely to save him—one man on a blown horse against a small army.

"Let's go, boy," he whispered, touching his heels to the roan's flanks and starting forward again along the wash's sandy bottom.

After a couple hundred yards of slow riding, not wanting to risk the roan on the uncertain terrain, he turned down a left fork in the wash. He remained in the wash, where the occasional mesquites, pin oaks, and greasewood shrubs shielded him from view from the open country, but when he came to an old, abandoned settler's cabin, he left the wash and rode toward a low range of hills humping against the stars in the east.

According to Hall, on the other side of those hills he'd find the Corpus ranch headquarters.

Before continuing, however, he stopped in the shack's

scrub-covered yard. Hall had told him he'd find fresh water in the covered well. When Longarm had dismounted the roan and loosened its saddle girth so it could drink and blow, he turned the wooden winch handle, but stopped suddenly, wincing, when a squawk sounded from the pulley.

Hall had told him the Corpus riders maintained the well, but apparently that didn't include oiling the winch. Stooped over the well, Longarm looked around cautiously. Spying no movement, and hearing no signs of anyone around the abandoned, mud-brick, tin-roofed shack or corrals or dilapidated hay barn, he continued to slowly turn the crank, until he had a leaky wooden bucket sitting on the ground before the thirsty roan.

While the roan drank, Longarm walked around, carefully scrutinizing his surroundings. The wash he'd left was a shaggy line of scrub mesquite in the northwest, the leaves of the shrubs silvered by moonlight. To the east were the hills, but before the hills he had a flat plain to cross.

Fortunately, however, no one seemed to be shadowing him. If there were more rustlers out here, it seemed that he'd slipped past them. He could ride faster now, as the terrain was less rugged than before, and the moon would light his and the roan's way. With luck, he'd be pounding on the Corpus ranch lodge in an hour.

Longarm allowed the roan only a quarter bucket of water, as the horse was warm and they still had a four- or five-mile ride ahead. He dropped the bucket back into the well, then cranked it up again, to drink the cool, sweet liquid himself and fill his canteen.

Ffteen minutes later he was well beyond the abandoned ranchstead and heading toward the jog of low, dark hills. He'd just turned slightly north to avoid a copse of pin oaks, when something slammed into the ground beside him with a resolute plunk and a low twang.

The roan lurched with a start, bunching its back muscles.

The rifle crack reached Longarm's ears a second later, echoing flatly.

"Ah, shit!"

He ground his heels into the roan's flanks and looked behind. A hundred or so yards away, north of the abandoned ranch, a short, scraggly line of black smudges jostled down out of some low, pale bluffs, angling toward Longarm. Someone shouted something, and then two more shots sounded, one right after the other.

The distant rataplan of galloping hooves could be heard beneath those of the trotting roan.

Amidst the dark worm of approaching riders—there appeared five, maybe six—a gun flashed. The slug screeched through the air around Longarm's head and crunched into a pin oak trunk. Longarm put his head down and urged the roan ahead with more speed, cursing his luck.

Had the winch alerted the riders, or had they spied him crossing the long flat in the moonlight? Likely they'd been watching for one of his group to make a run for it after dark. They couldn't let even one get away to spill the beans on their rustling operation.

Longarm cursed again loudly and crouched even lower, aiming the roan toward a notch in the hills ahead and slightly right. The roan had been only moderately well rested when he'd left Hall and Tremaine, and so far Longarm had taken it easy, but now he could feel the fatigue in the horse's sluggish stride, hear the exhaustion in its raspy breathing.

Again, he fired a glance behind him. The riders were gradually gaining on him, all six spread out in a line, pistols or rifles winking in the darkness, the sharp cracks echoing off the hills. Longarm triggered a return shot, to try and hold them, but it only seemed to spur them harder, the shaggy line moving toward him more quickly and snapping off more shots.

Longarm had no ammunition to spare, so he holstered the Colt and kept his head down, trying to urge more speed from the roan but conjuring only harder, raspier breaths from the tired beast. The hill humped up larger before him. He turned the roan down a broad crease to the right, looking around wildly for a place to hole up. A dark line shone in the slope ahead and right. There was a mesquite there, too, and as Longarm approached the shrub he saw that the line was another fold in the hills.

He looked behind. His pursuers were out of sight behind a bend in the trail; he could hear them yelling, their horses' hooves thudding, but he couldn't see them. Quickly, wishing he had more time to investigate the route, he swung the roan into the crease on the other side of the moon-silvered mesquite. He was likely to find himself in a box canyon or a bobcat den, but he had to chance it. With luck, the riders would ride on past the opening, and keep riding. With more luck, he'd lose them, find a back door to the gap, and then find a good place to hole up for an hour or two until the roan had regained its wind.

The roan stumbled as it negotiated the narrow gap between two boulders that had long ago rolled down from the slopes above. Longarm planted a boot on the sheer wall of the bluff to his left, steadying the beast, then returned his boot to the stirrup as the horse continued forward into the crease that was as dark as the inside of a black glove on a foggy night.

The cool air smelled of stone and sage, and the breeze

rustled faintly through the chasm. On the hill above and right, the leaves of a hackberry rattled, and the spindly branches made a scratching sound. From behind, Longarm heard the faint clomp of hooves and distant voices.

His heart lightened slightly when the sounds grew fainter. Had the gang ridden on past the mouth of the narrow gap, like he'd hoped?

"I couldn't be that lucky," he growled as the roan continued nervously forward, deeper and deeper into the black defile. "Not on this job."

He was right. He couldn't be that lucky.

He found that out ten minutes later, when the dark canyon ahead of him turned even darker. Black, in fact. His heart thumped as the shamble-footed roan continued forward. He squinted into the darkness, hoping that the flat blackness he was staring ahead at wasn't the solid wall it appeared to be.

To no avail.

He reined the roan to a stop. There was just enough light for him to see the chalky wall ahead of him, showing streaks and patches of black volcanic stone beneath the pale brown dirt, standing nearly straight up and down, and stretching a good hundred feet above his head. The loose gravel at the horse's feet told him there was probably a spring in here, likely at the base of the wall, though it probably ran for only a few weeks every year.

Or maybe not at all anymore. At one time a good amount of water had carved out this canyon. A box canyon.

A man trap.

The phrase had no sooner passed through Longarm's mind than he heard echoing hoof clomps behind him. A voice rose, then another—both pitched in frustration and anger.

Longarm unsnapped the keeper thong over his holster and pulled the Colt free. So not only had he run into the box canyon he'd feared, but the gun wolves had cut his trail into it.

He swung down from the saddle and looked around. The clomping and the voices grew louder. When Longarm had found a narrow, rock-strewn trough in the canyon wall to his left, he hurried back to the horse, aimed it down the dark defile, and slapped the Colt's butt against the animal's ass.

"*Go!*"

The roan gave a halfhearted buck and shambled back the way it had come, on an interception course with the oncoming gun wolves. The roan might delay the group for a few seconds by blocking the passage, long enough to give Longarm time to make it at least halfway up the trough, with a good start toward the star-capped rim. There was no point in trying to shoot it out down here in the canyon. He might be able to take the first couple riders, but the others would drill him so full of holes he'd look like a target can.

He holstered the Colt and scrambled up the gravelly trough. There was a thin covering of dirt over the black lava rock, and the gravel was thick and loose in places, making it a tough climb. But he concentrated on each step, keeping one eye skinned on the murky-dark canyon floor below, and one on the starry sky beckoning above.

If he could get out of here and hole up somewhere in the hills, he might have a chance . . .

He'd barely gotten started when the yelling from up the gap grew shriller, louder. Horses whinnied, and there was a great scraping of shod hooves on stone.

Longarm grinned. The cutthroats had run into the roan.

A man shouted hoarsely, partly obscured by echoes in

the narrow chasm: "Don't shoot it, Morgan! He'll block the damn corridor!"

As the shouting and scrambling continued below, Longarm moved as quickly as he could on the slippery dirt and gravel, crabbing on his hands and feet and sometimes his knees when his feet slid out from beneath him. He grabbed small brush clumps and fixed rocks to pull himself up.

Below, the hoof clomps and voices grew louder.

Longarm was halfway to the top of the trough, feeling the cool night air flowing down to meet him, when the horse clomps grew to a ringing crescendo directly beneath him. He could hear the squawk and rattle of tack, and the labored, frenetic breaths of men and animals.

"He's gotta be here!" someone shouted, the voice so clear that it seemed to originate from just behind Longarm's head.

"Can't see a damn thing!"

A pistol popped three times. The reports in the cramped confines smacked Longarm's ears like cupped hands.

"Goddamnit, Morgan, you're gonna pink one of us with a rico—"

"Up there!" another cutthroat shouted, cutting the other man off. "He's climbin' the wall!"

Guns popped.

Bullets spanged off the slope on both sides of Longarm. He quickened his pace, and snaked a hand over the top of the trough. Several more shots hammered from below, hot lead sizzling around Longarm's ears and pinging off the ridge. One sliced across the back of his thigh—an icy, stinging burn that stretched his lips back from his teeth.

He'd begun pulling himself the last few feet to the ridge's lip, when a bullet tore through the back of his arm, flooding him with a grinding, white-hot heat. The blow hammered the air from his lungs. As he tried to suck it back, his left hand released the knob of rock he'd just grabbed and had begun pulling with.

He fell so quickly and violently, the ridge rolling up beneath him in a dark brown blur as rocky knobs and dry brush clumps pummeled him mercilessly, that when he hit the canyon floor on his back, he was still flailing with his hands as though reaching for the rim.

Silence. Dust sifted. Gravel clattered to the floor.

As if from far away, someone laughed.

Longarm opened his eyes. Silhouetted faces stared down at him.

"What should we do now?" someone asked.

There was another pregnant silence.

Longarm heard himself sort of mewl and groan softly as he tried to suck a breath into his battered torso. He felt as though he'd been pierced with multiple arrows, broken over a wagon tongue, and staked to an anthill in the desert sun for several hot summer days.

A match flicked to life. The man holding it crouched low over Longarm. No, not a man. The match flame caressed over the tawny face of a dark-eyed, clean-jawed woman in man's clothes, including a dusty, green stockman's hat with a feather and a Texas crease.

She wore a striped blouse, several buttons of which were undone. The lace edge of a camisole shone just below the deep V of the woman's cleavage, pushing outward as the two nice-sized breasts swelled against the shirt with the woman's breathing.

The two large brown eyes flashed like copper in the light of the match flame. They followed Longarm's gaze to the well-filled shirt. Looking at Longarm again, the girl curled her upper lip.

"Kill him." She straightened and walked away, boots grinding gravel.

Longarm threw a hand toward her, as if to stop her, to hold her back, but it was like throwing a smithy's iron anvil. His entire throbbing left arm weighed as much as a boxcar.

He loosed a raspy exhalation, eyelids closing, and was consumed by burning, aching darkness.

# Chapter 13

When Longarm awakened, he was not only surprised that he was alive, lying in a big, comfortable bed in a room dancing with wan lantern light and misty shadows, but that someone was sucking his cock.

And doing a pretty damn good job of it.

All he could see of the girl was her hair. Thick, dark brown tresses cascaded over her face to lie in a silky, lantern-burnished pile on his naked belly. As she bobbed her head, running her warm, wet mouth and expert tongue up and down his blood-engorged length, he could see his mast standing proud and hard, like an obsequious, disloyal cur who, when its owner is absent, throws itself at the feet of the first friendly face that comes along.

Longarm looked around the room but found it difficult to take in anything but the sensations below his waist—the girl's mouth and tongue and the light caress of her pillowing hair. The wet sounds of her sucking mingled with the occasional sputter of the lantern on the table beside him.

All he knew was that he was in a big four-poster with a feather-filled mattress under a herringbone-patterned ceiling hewn from hand-adzed pine logs. And that he was getting some of the best fellatio he'd experienced in the last ten years. Aside from that—how he'd gotten here, how long he'd been here, and what condition he was in— he had no idea and couldn't for the life of him bring himself to care.

When he'd first awakened, he'd been close to climax, and he hadn't the strength to hold himself back. The girl sensed his passion peaking, and really hunkered down to the workbench, so to speak, placing both her fine-boned hands on his hip bones to steady herself.

She finished him off good and proper, and lapped him clean. She released his dwindling cock, and it slapped wetly against his belly.

When she lifted her head, breathing hard and running the back of her hand across her mouth, Longarm saw the last image that had been blazed across his retinas before unconsciousness grabbed him back in the night-choked box canyon.

Only this time she wasn't wearing a shirt.

Despite the searing pain that was beginning to make itself known, Longarm felt his mouth corners rise. The girl's wide, brown eyes met his, and her lower jaw dropped. A lacy camisole was bunched around her waist. She reached down quickly, pulled it up to cover her large, well-formed, dark-tipped breasts, and lurched forward to blow out the lantern.

Dark like the bottom of a deep mine pit filled the room.

"You're dreaming!" the girl said, breathless.

Longarm couldn't see her in the new dark, but he heard bare feet padding across the wooden floor. A door clicked, hinges squawked, and then the door clicked again. Beyond the door, there were the light thumps of her running on the balls of her feet, with the occasional squawk of a floorboard.

Then silence.

Longarm lay back against his pillow, smelling the kerosene mixing with the lingering, feminine smell of the girl, which assured him he hadn't been dreaming. Confusion swept him as keenly as had bliss only a moment before, as acutely as the burning pain all through him and especially in his upper left arm.

Finally, he released all the questions and let sleep swath him once more.

When Longarm woke again, he was just as disoriented as he had been the first time he'd gained consciousness in the strange room.

Only this time it was morning, with golden sunshine angling through the room's two sashed windows covered by thin, wash-worn curtains. He'd been awakened by voices and movements below him.

Pushing up on his elbows, he had a vague recollection of awakening the first time to the sensation of feminine lips locked around his cock. The recollection gained more solidity as he looked around groggily, smacking his dry lips and feeling as though a half dozen caterpillars had crawled down his throat and died while coiled around his tonsils.

His body ached and burned, and his head swam. It was as though there were a filter over his brain, allowing only a few half-formed thoughts to penetrate at a time. He knew who he was and, for some reason, that he was in Texas. But beyond that and the girl, who may or may not have been conjured by his damaged noggin, he couldn't remember shit.

He dropped his gaze to the star quilt covering him. Certainly, he'd dreamt the blow job. But then he remembered the face of the girl staring up at him from around his crotch—those full lips and dark brown eyes—and he put that face together with the face of the girl he suddenly remembered seeing in the canyon.

Longarm shook his head.

The canyon.

What canyon? Had he dreamt that, too?

He glanced at the nearest window, at a small charcoal brazier huddled in the far corner, with a scoop and an apple crate mounded with charcoal beside it. He shuttled his gaze to the door, to which a coyote pelt was nailed, and then at the small table abutting the wall right of the door. A straight-backed chair was pushed up to the table, and his clothes—they appeared freshly laundered—hung over the chair's back.

His pistol belt was there, too. His revolver jutted from the holster, visible beneath a sleeve of his black frock coat.

He slowly, purposefully, digested all these details, as though in one or more of them, or maybe in all of them together, he could remember where he was and what had brought him here. But before he could get a solid grasp of the answers he was after, he became aware of his swollen bladder.

He sucked a sharp breath and grabbed his crotch. He glanced under the bed, sucking another breath as the movement aggravated the heavy, throbbing pain in his left arm. He saw a thin, porcelain-coated thunder mug sitting, covered, just under the bed. With effort, he tossed the bedcovers away and was vaguely surprised to find that he was buck naked—who had undressed him? the girl?—but not at all surprised to see that he was liberally mottled with scabbed scrapes and deep purple bruises.

The way he ached, throbbed, and burned all over, he was surprised he wasn't black from the toes up.

Well, the bruises pretty well validated the canyon memory. Before he could concentrate on anything else, he had to evacuate his bladder before he popped a seam or two.

He dropped his feet to the floor and slowly, breathing hard and grunting against the pain in his swollen piss pocket, kicked the thunder mug out from under the bed and used his right big toe to remove the lid. As the lid clattered to the floor, he spread his feet in front of the empty pot.

The room pitched and rolled. Longarm cursed, threw himself forward, and used the bed to steady himself. Keeping one hand on the bed's edge, he used his other hand to aim his dong, and let go.

*"Ahhhhh!"*

In this position, and with the room rocking like a hammock on a windy Dakota afternoon, he had a hard time keeping his stream on target. He dribbled a little over the sides. But the sweet bliss of satisfaction filled him in direct proportion to the long-held fluid leaving him, and his taut muscles relaxed.

By the time he'd finally drained himself dry, he was exhausted and almost sobbing with relief. His overstrained knees were buckling, so instead of trying to stand, he merely slumped forward onto the bed and rolled onto his back, keeping his feet on the floor until he could summon the strength to lift them.

He drew several deep breaths and turned his head to look at his arm. The upper part of the limb was wrapped with a thick, cotton bandage. A little blood shone in the front. The bullet must have gone all the way through, from back to front, but it must be heal—

Longarm lifted his head suddenly as remembered images flooded back to him.

Hall and Tremaine!

Heart thumping, Longarm ground his heels into the floor, shoved his elbows into the bed, and heaved himself to his feet.

Too fast.

As he staggered drunkenly forward, the far wall pitched toward him like the neck of a bucking bronc. The scarred wooden floor flew up and smacked him so hard about his face, chest, and shoulders that he half-consciously suspected that he could now add a shattered beak to his list of ailments.

He groaned.

He couldn't hear much beyond the groan and the ringing in his ears, but he thought he could hear alarmed voices somewhere in the house. He felt vibrations in the floor that was cold and rough against his palms, his thighs, and his right cheek.

The room's door burst open, and a girl ran in.

"It's him, Pa-pa!" she yelled as she ran toward Longarm and dropped to both knees on the floor beside him. The same girl in the canyon, the same one from his wet dream. "What on earth are you doing, mister? Trying to kill yourself?"

As she placed her hands on his right arm, a stocky, older gent shambled in behind her. "What the hell? *Dios mío, hombre!*"

"Horses," Longarm gritted out, pushing up onto his hands and getting a bruised knee under him. "I need a couple horses. Left . . . two men out in the rimrocks."

"Let's get him back into bed, Ana," the man grunted, dropping to a knee on Longarm's left side and wrapping an arm around his waist.

"*Sí,*" the girl grunted as, together, she and the old gent pulled Longarm to his feet.

He tried to protest, but they somehow at once hustled

and gentled him back over to the bed and sat him down. They both had hard jaws and no-nonsense eyes, and Longarm's feeble complaints fell on deaf ears until they had him lying prostrate on the bed and covered with a thin sheet and the star quilt.

"You are going nowhere until you heal, Marshal Long," the gent said, standing over the bed and looking severe.

He was a short, rotund Mexican, balding, with slicked-back hair on the sides and a few stubborn salt-and-pepper strands on top. His walrus mustache was waxed, his boots polished, and his short charro jacket, crisp white shirt, and turquoise-studded bolo tie were impeccable.

"I am Miguel Corpus. This is my daughter, Ana. My men and daughter ran you down by mistake. They thought you were one of Woolyard's hired guns from Pleasant Valley . . . until they saw your badge lying in the dirt where you fell."

Corpus cast an admonishing glance at the girl called Ana, whose own, vaguely defiant gaze did not flicker. "Sometimes my daughter gets a little overzealous. It's living out here, I guess . . . so close to the Pleasant Valley cutthroats. Nevertheless, your injuries are my responsibility, señor. I read through your identifying papers. I know who you are. And I don't wish to lock horns with the federal government."

"Like I said, damnit," Longarm said, raising his hands to his head and realizing for the first time that a bandage encircled it, "I left two men in the lava bluffs about fifteen miles northeast. A stock detective and a Texas Ranger."

"What were you doing in the lava bluffs? It's good for nothing but coyotes and rattlesnakes, and not too many of those."

"I was looking into the rustling, hoping to put an end to

the Pleasant Valley War." Longarm wasn't convinced that Miguel Corpus wasn't involved in the long-looping, but if he were, Longarm doubted he, Longarm, would still be breathing, however painfully, in the rancher's own guest room.

"I and Hall and Tremaine stumbled into them rattlesnakes you mentioned, and there's more than you think. The human kind. With long, well-used lariats." Longarm squinted an eye at the man standing a few feet from his comely, dark-haired, dark-eyed daughter. "Wouldn't happen to know anything about that, would you?"

Corpus scrunched up his round, weathered face, gave a frustrated growl, and swung toward the door. "Tend him, Ana. Get him well, put him on his horse, and get him out of here!"

"Hold on!" Longarm tried to yell. It came out as an embarrassingly feeble croak.

Corpus stopped at the door and swung back toward Longarm, placing one hand on the door frame. His ruddy face was flushed. "You've been here four days, señor. If the rustlers had Tremaine and Hall pinned down, their bones have been licked clean by now. I would send some men to bring back what is left, but I have only three at the headquarters, as the other eight are moving cattle in from Sand River. I need three here in case I get trouble from Pleasant Valley."

Corpus wheeled and disappeared.

The girl leaned down and adjusted Longarm's pillow beneath his head, jerking it around with a tad too much vigor, making Longarm's head throb harder. He was aware of two goose eggs—one sprouting from his right temple, one at the back of his head, just above his hat line. He wasn't sure which one had the larger, throbbing heart in it.

The girl wasn't trying to abuse him with her pillow-jostling; Longarm could see by her eyes. She was just a vigorous girl. Overzealous, in her father's word. From her skin tone, Longarm judged she was Mexican, like her father, but with a little Indian blood, as well. A *mestizo*. She'd been raised around *americanos*, however, for she spoke with only a slight Spanish accent.

When she'd finished with the pillow, she said, "Would you like something to eat?"

Longarm was about to shake his head. His stomach felt like a nest of wriggling snakes and worms. But then he figured he'd heal faster, be able to get back on the trail for the rimrock country quicker, if he had food.

Likely the girl's father was right—Hall and Tremaine were probably dead. But Longarm had to find out.

"Got any broth?"

"Antelope stew."

"That'll do."

"How about some tortillas? And coffee?"

"I'll give it a shot," he said, suddenly all too aware of his quivering gut.

"I'll be right back," the girl said. She set the cover on the chamber pot, lifted the pot by its wire handle, and turning, headed for the door, her flowered calico skirt swirling about her legs and ripe, round hips.

She was wearing moccasins and a loose cotton blouse that, despite his condition, Longarm couldn't help noticing was nicely filled. Her ankles, between the tops of her moccasins and the bottom of the red-and-black skirt, were light cherry tan.

"You . . . uh . . ." His voice stopped her. One hand on the doorknob, she turned to him.

"You weren't in here last night, were you?" At least, he thought it was last night when he'd awakened in unexpected carnal bliss, but as badly as his brains were scrambled, it could have been any of the past four.

Her eyes widened slightly. Was that a flush rising in her cheeks?

She laughed and said, "I have come into your room every night since you've been here. To make sure you didn't need anything. Did I wake you?"

Longarm narrowed a suspicious eye, glancing quickly at his clothes on the chair. "Who undressed me?"

"Why, me, of course. I also helped you with the chamber pot." She paused, staring at him, her hand nervously twisting the doorknob behind her. "Would you have preferred Pa-Pa had done it . . . or his men?"

Longarm relaxed his head against the pillow. "Just wonderin'." Then he thought of something else. "You always ride at night in the hills yonder with your father's rannies?"

"*Sí*. Often I do." A little smirk quirked one side of her mouth. "I was taught to be as good with cattle as any of them." She glanced at the .44 jutting from Longarm's holster hanging on the chair. "And as good with a gun, too. Not many women survive out here who aren't good at both."

"You got a ma?"

The girl glanced away for just a second, and one eye narrowed slightly as though with a pain twinge. "Killed by Comanches."

"Sorry."

"It was long ago. I hardly remember." Her eyes slid back to him. "Any more questions, Marshal Long?"

Longarm dropped his own gaze to the foot of the bed. "I reckon that'll do for now."

"I'll be back."

Ana Corpus turned and left, and Longarm's eyes followed her shapely ass out of the room.

# Chapter 14

The door latch clicked.

Longarm opened his eyes.

He couldn't see anything in the dark room in spite of a cool, blue shaft of moonlight snaking through one of the windows. His hand had just drifted toward the Colt he had hung from a front bedpost when a familiar voice whispered, "Custis?"

This was the second night after his post-piss fall on the Corpus guest room floor, and Longarm and Ana had gotten on a first-name basis. He pushed up on his elbows. "Still here, I reckon, though I figure to push on tomorrow."

Door hinges squeaked faintly, and a slender shadow moved into the room. "It is midnight, and I'm getting ready to turn in," she said. "I was just checking to make sure you didn't need anything."

She was lit from behind by a guttering, red-chimneyed bracket lamp down the hall, probably outside her own room, though Longarm hadn't left the guest room to gain a sense of the lodge's layout. He could sense, however, that the house was far more modest than the Woolyard residence though he preferred the smell of this place—the aroma of spiced meats and breads and chicory-laced coffee wafting up from the kitchen below.

She closed the door softly. The old man was probably asleep somewhere, and she obviously didn't want to wake him. Longarm didn't say anything, but waited for her to materialize out of the room's shadowy darkness and stop before him. The moonlight touched one side of her curly brown hair. It limned her flaring nose, firm lips, and round chin. It touched a small pendant dangling down the front of her embroidered, scoop-necked blouse, to hang just above the valley between her breasts.

Longarm took a deep breath—something he hadn't been able to do because of his bruised chest until recently—and liked what he smelled. The vaguely spicy, fruity scent of her was especially strong this evening.

Slowly, only a little louder than before, she said, "Are you hungry? Thirsty? Do you still have water?"

Longarm had been sleeping so much that just now he'd only been dozing, and he felt good enough to have a little fun. Snaking an arm behind his head, he said, "Remember the other night, when you told me I was dreamin'?"

Her voice was tentative, skeptical. "Yes. I mean . . . no, I don't know what you're talking about!"

"You sorta had me guessin' there for a while," Longarm said. "But I think most of my senses—at least, what I had to begin with—have come back to me. And if you weren't doin' something dirty to me the other night, back in the way, way middle of the night, when dear old Pa-pa was sawin' up logs into kindlin' and tinder, I was born on the far side of the moon in a stardust manger."

Longarm's eyes having adjusted to the moonlit darkness, he could see her better now. Her throat moved as she swallowed, and her voice was at once hard and sharp as, turning toward the door, she said, "Well, I see you need nothing, so I will stop."

"What's the matter—don't like suckin' on a man who's wide awake and can enjoy it thoroughly?"

She turned back to him. Her voice was so throaty and raspy as to be almost inaudible. "I am not a pervert. You were swollen, that's all, and . . . and I thought I would help . . . help relieve your need."

"Might have done it with your hand." Longarm chuckled but kept his voice just above a whisper as he watched the girl's breasts rise and fall behind the low-cut blouse, making the pendant jostle faintly. "Instead you had me down around your tonsils. That ain't just givin' medicinal attention, Ana Corpus. That's a girl who likes to have a man now and then . . . maybe when the old man ain't lookin'. But I got a feelin' he's damn near always lookin'."

The corners of Longarm's mouth lifted, and he felt his mustache brush his nose. "But he ain't lookin' now. And I'm wide awake enough to appreciate a girl's natural talents."

He doubted the talents were purely natural, however. No girl who gave a blow job like the one she'd given him the other night could do so without practice. He didn't hold it against her. Like Verna Woolyard out at Pleasant Valley, Ana Corpus was likely lonely and, being a healthy girl, she had certain needs every bit as strong as those of the gunmen who worked for her pa.

"*Dios,*" she said breathily, dropping her chin. "I am . . . embarrassed." She moved forward and sat slowly down on the edge of the bed. She stared at him, the moon reflected in her brown eyes. After a time, she laid a hand on the star quilt, pressed it down on his erection. "I was helping you with the chamber pot, but you couldn't go because—"

"I've discovered that in situations like these," Longarm interrupted her as he threw the covers back to expose his fully engorged shaft, "it's best to do as little talkin' as possible. So how 'bout you take that pretty little blouse off, hike up your skirt, climb on up here on the bed, and take you another mouthful like you did the other night, while I'm still awake, so I can give it the full appreciation it deserves?"

Longarm saw her brows knit slightly and her lips purse. She didn't like being ordered around. Likely, out in the bunkhouse or wherever she met up with her father's hands, she did the bossing. Her breasts rose and fell slowly, and then she grabbed the bottom of her blouse with both hands and lifted it up and over her head. As her hair danced in rich swirls about her shoulders, she held the blouse out to one side, letting it swing there for a few seconds, as if she was still considering—or wanting to consider—whether or not to proceed.

Her fingers opened. The blouse fluttered to the floor with a soft rustle. Still sitting on the edge of the bed, one leg curled under the other, she slowly lifted her skirt up around her waist, laying her legs bare and revealing the fact that she wasn't wearing underclothes.

Longarm reached forward, ran his hand along a shapely thigh and her right butt cheek, dipping one finger into the crack and angling it forward. She rose up slightly with a gasp, and then she swallowed and turned her head toward his member—mast-straight and angling back over his belly. As Longarm's fingers probed the moistness of her furred snatch under and between her crossed legs, she reached out slowly, wrapped a hand around his cock, and squeezed it gently.

Longarm bunched his lips at the touch. His heart fluttered.

She ran her hand slowly up and down his engorged dong, continuing to squeeze it like a dairy farmer manipulates a sore teat. At the same time, Longarm tickled the edges of her pussy, working up a wetness there and causing her to shift slightly, lift her ass a little, and spread her thighs another inch more.

Ana groaned. Her breathing came fast. Her pebbling nipples caught the moonlight.

Gradually, she pumped Longarm's cock harder, until finally she fairly threw herself on top of it. Instantly, he felt the warm wetness of her mouth engulf him and saw her head moving around on his crotch as she sucked him with savage passion, spreading her legs farther to give him better access to her pussy.

She groaned and sucked, groaned and sucked, the wet cracking and popping sounds adding to the allure and causing every nerve in Longarm's body to fly down to his member, where as one they coiled, popped, hissed, and had him grinding his teeth and arching his back in a bittersweet fight to contain himself.

When she had the fountain all but ready to gush, the heat of her mouth was suddenly gone. The saliva remaining on his cock quickly turned cool. His nerves sparked and slithered like lightning-struck snakes just beneath the skin of the enflamed love organ.

He opened his eyes, frowning. She scooted up toward him, lifting her snatch off his fingers and sliding one knee across his belly, straddling him.

She lowered her lips to his, stuck her tongue into his mouth, entangling it with his tongue, then running it across his teeth. When she lifted her head, he placed his hands on her swollen breasts, rolling the projecting nipples under his thumbs. Her orbs were hard as cantaloupes and slick with a fine sweat sheen.

"I want it in me," she rasped damply against his chin.

She lifted her butt and looked down between them, grabbing his iron-hard member in one hand and slipping it into her dripping portal. Gasping, she lifted her head sharply, then gritted her teeth and gave a shiver, as though a door to a below-zero winter evening had suddenly blown open.

Desperately, she took his face between her hands and cried, "I'll be gentle—I promise, oh, *Cristo!*"

"Don't bother," Longarm groaned.

Digging her fingers into Longarm's slablike pectoral muscles, she shook her hair off of her face, drew a deep breath, and began rocking back and forth on her knees. She started slowly, riding him like she would a freshly broken colt. But as her fingers dug deeper and deeper into his bruised chest, she quickened her pace into a plunging attack. The bed squawked and barked, but she was obviously practiced enough—and knew well enough how deeply her father slept—that she kept the commotion to a low roar.

After the plundering that left them both sweating, tense, and rigid, with Longarm pushing up on his elbows and squeezing her tender ass in both his calloused hands, she slowed her movements to a rock until shifting all her weight to her knees and grinding against him for the long, hard, roiling finale.

Longarm loosed a lengthy, relieved sigh as a gauzy, postcoital cloud rose up to receive him.

Ana lowered her face to his and scrunched up her cheeks into a bizarre mask of rapturous, otherworldly passion.

Slowly, as her soaked snatch quivered and expanded around his slackening member, the muscles in her face relaxed, and groaning and whimpering with the dying after-shocks, she slumped against him. She lay like that, softly snoring into his shoulder, until he'd gained enough strength to roll her onto her back.

He kissed her breasts, her nose, her lips, and chin, then fell back against the pillow, asleep before he'd drawn a complete breath.

Sometime during the night, so quietly that Longarm hadn't awakened, Ana slipped out of the guest room. When Long-arm awakened at the first blush of dawn—relieved to see that after four days of having his days and nights shuffled his inner alarm clock was still functioning—only the girl's alluring smell and her body's indentation in the bed be-spoke her presence.

That and a somewhat raw and sticky sensation in Long-arm's nether regions.

He crawled out of bed and tested his walking ability. He was still stiff and sore, but the little man in his head had eased up with his hammer, and he managed a couple of passes around the room and a long piss in the chamber pot without falling. So after a quick whore's bath, he dressed, shouldered his saddlebags and war bag, and followed the spicy scent of a Mexican-style breakfast down a rough-hewn staircase to the house's first story.

As Longarm followed the smells and the clatter of pots and pans toward the kitchen, he saw that the house was indeed humble in size, but well appointed with comfortable furniture and animal rugs. There was a large fieldstone hearth in the parlor, along with Mexican blankets draped over the leather armchairs and couches. The hearth was cold now, but aromatic Mexican cigar smoke and the piney scent of many fires lingered.

"Ah, Señor Long," Ana said when Longarm stopped in the low-beamed entrance to the kitchen. "How nice to see you up and around."

She was sitting at a round table with her father, both crouched over oval-shaped breakfast plates while a skinny Mexican in baggy jeans and long, braided hair flipped flapjacks at a heavy iron range.

Longarm shifted the gear on his shoulders. "It's nice to *be* up and around. I reckon I'm ready to ride." He glanced at Miguel Corpus, who sat looking up at Longarm with a scowl furling his bushy gray brows. "I hate to be even more of a burden than I have been, señor," Longarm said, "but I'd appreciate your lending me a couple horses. A rifle, too, and some ammunition if you can spare it. My pistol's a forty-four."

Corpus chuffed caustically, tossed an arm out in a dismissive gesture, and continued shoveling huevos rancheros into his mouth.

"Please sit down," Ana said, rising from her chair. "I will get a plate."

"Thanks but no thanks, Miss Corpus," Longarm said formally, for the benefit of the girl's father. Dealing with women you'd gotten down and dirty with was awkward enough the morning after without having to deal with their fathers, as well. "I best be hitting the trail . . . with those two horses."

"I will send Philipe out for the horses," Corpus said gruffly. "Though why you intend to head back into those rimrocks, I have no idea. Those men are dead. But first, sit down and fill your belly, Marshal Long. Now, after such injuries as you sustained, is not the time to be starting out on an empty belly."

Ana had already taken down a plate from a cupboard

and gone to the stove, where the skinny Mexican promptly shoveled food onto it. When Ana had placed a *bizcocho*—a moist but spicy bun—onto the steaming plate and set the plate on the table, Longarm's belly rumbled. When she'd set a stone mug of smoking coffee in front of the plate and the aroma of chicory rose on the steam, his belly kicked like a startled milch cow, and he found himself dropping his gear onto a free chair, kicking out the one in front of his plate, and sinking into it.

"Much obliged," he told the girl, who'd retaken her place across from him.

She looked at him demurely, then glanced at her father. His brows still rumpled with disapproval, Miguel Corpus's attention was on his food. Ana looked back at Longarm and let a lascivious grin slide across her face before dropping her attention to her own food.

# Chapter 15

Longarm's ears warmed at the girl's brazen look with her father in the room.

"Much obliged for the grub, señorita."

He hunkered over his plate and didn't realize until he was swabbing the last of the runny yoke and beans with a spicy bun that he hadn't looked up all the short time he'd been eating.

Looking up now, he saw both Ana and her father regarding him ironically.

"Philipe," the old man said, turning to the cook, who was scrubbing out one of the pans.

"*Sí, jefe?*" the man said, turning toward the table and bowing his long head with its horsey, droopy-eyed face.

Corpus spoke so quickly that Longarm's rudimentary understanding of Spanish made it hard to follow. But the lawman thought that, ensconced in his orders to Philipe to saddle a couple of spare horses in addition to Longarm's roan, and to furnish a rifle and ammunition, he'd called Longarm a foolish, bullheaded gringo and a few other things possibly even less complimentary. Longarm's suspicions were corroborated by a smirk from Ana over the rim of her coffee mug and by the eyes of the cook, whose gaze swept Longarm fleetingly as, bowing and nodding to his employer, he grabbed a battered old sombrero off a peg by the door and hustled outside.

Ana poured Longarm a fresh cup of coffee, and he sank back in his chair to await the horses and to dig a cigar from his shirt pocket. "I'd think you'd be right grateful I was riding back into them rimrocks, Mr. Corpus," he said, scratching a match to life on his belt buckle. He touched the match to the cheroot—the first one he'd had in days—and exhaled smoke through his nostrils. "If I can get a handle on whoever's rustling Pleasant Valley beef, I might be able to put an end to the Pleasant Valley War."

Corpus had sunk back in his own chair to puff his own stogie while Ana cleared the table, regarding the men warily, as though they were two old mossyhorns she might need to separate to prevent a wrecked corral. "They are not stealing my beef," Corpus growled. "Only Pleasant Valley beef. May they steal them all! Let it be the end of Pleasant Valley!"

"Once they finish off Pleasant Valley," Longarm pointed out, "they might just get started on you and the other ranchers who filed claims on state school land."

Corpus pounded the table and gritted his teeth. "I did not file claims on state school land! My land is part of an old Spanish land grant—willed to me by my grandfather. Only, after the War and more settlers moved into this country, the Texas courts refused to uphold it and forced me—if I was to stay here where I had already built my *ranchería*—to go through the formalities of filing their state school land leases. A charade, and a grave insult to me and to my forefathers!"

"Pa-Pa," Ana said, squeezing the spindles of her father's chair back and looking down at him beseechingly. "It is not good to get so worked up."

Corpus shook his head and cursed softly in Spanish.

"I'm sorry, Corpus," Longarm said. "But that's a little out of my jurisdiction. And well beyond my expertise. Sounds like you need a good lawyer."

"*Sí, sí.* I need a good lawyer. But a good lawyer requires money, and after all the drought years, and now the war with Pleasant Valley, even my credit in Claireville is good for only about ten pounds of pinto beans."

He sighed as he reached up to pat his daughter's placating hand lingering on his chair back. "What is the difference? Woolyard will not rest until I am driven out, anyway."

"Might help to clear you of rustling charges," Longarm said, hearing the rattle of bridle chains and the slow clomp of horses growing louder outside the cabin's front door.

"That is of little consideration anymore, Marshal Long."

Corpus blew a thick smoke cloud at the ceiling as Ana returned to the steaming washtub on the cook range. The old man's eyes were rheumy with emotion.

"Woolyard killed off all my good men months ago, when the rustling first started. He just assumed I was responsible without bothering to ride out and speak to me civilly, man-to-man. Now, knowing of the danger, few good vaqueros will ride for me. Those who remain are loyal, but they are few, and I need them all for cattle work, not running down rustlers or dying at the hands of Woolyard's hired gunmen."

"Well, I've put a ten-day moratorium on the war," Longarm said as he climbed to his feet, wincing at the rake of his shirt and trousers against his still-raw scrapes and abrasions. "If you and him'll give me a chance, maybe I can work some magic out here."

His cheerful tone belied his apprehension. Obviously, Corpus and Woolyard harbored a deep-seated animosity that was not likely to go away when the real culprits of the cattle thievery had been run to ground. They were sort of like old, mule-headed mutts that would fight over supper bones long after the bones themselves had been buried and forgotten.

But it was a start.

"One man?" Corpus laughed as he ran his eyes up and down Longarm's impressive frame. "Even an *hombre grande* like you, Marshal Long, cannot round up all the rustlers that must be holing up in the lava bluffs. No, no, no. You go up there, and you will end up like your friends."

"You never know." Longarm settled his gear on his shoulders. "My friends might still be kickin' out there somewheres."

"What is the old *americano* saying?" Corpus said, flashing large yellow teeth as he stared through his cigar smoke at the ceiling. "If wishes had wings, pigs would fly!"

Longarm glanced at Ana, touched a forefinger to his hat brim, and headed outside to where three horses including his roan stood waiting for him. The long-haired Mexican was still going over them, adjusting the tack.

As he rode out of the yard a few minutes later, Longarm glanced back to see Ana and old Corpus standing outside the cabin, watching him. Old Corpus had his arms crossed on his chest, and he was slowly, ominously shaking his head.

Longarm had been able to see the low, dark bulk of the lava bluffs humping up in the distance from the guest room window, so he hadn't bothered asking Corpus for a map. Now, as he headed toward that broken country, hoping he'd find Hall and Tremaine alive, the creased and gouged southeastern sides of the dark hills were brushed pink and lemon as the sun nudged the eastern horizon, painting the high, thin clouds over Longarm's head a glowing rose.

The air was cool, the ground damp with dew. Piping birds flitted here and there about the spindly brush. Cows dotted the landscape, and occasionally one gave a raucous, mule-like bellow.

As Longarm negotiated the low, jumbled hills, meandering northwest, the bulk of Corpus's herd fell away behind him, and the morning heated up, so that he shrugged out of his Prince Albert frock coat and tied it around his bedroll. Confident he was heading back the way he'd come—as he'd passed the old ranchstead where he'd drawn water up from the well just before Ana and the Corpus riders had ridden him to ground—he withdrew the Winchester carbine from the saddle boot.

He worked the cocking lever. The gun was in good shape. Not as good shape as his own '73, but it was fully loaded and well oiled, and since he'd left his own rifle with Tremaine, it would have to do. He aimed from his shoulder, picking out a dog cactus, then a jackrabbit hightailing it around a mesquite shrub, and then lowered the gun. He wouldn't know till he fired it, but the sights seemed in line and the barrel was straight.

Returning the rifle to the saddle boot, he pulled his .44 from his holster. He'd filled his cartridge belt from the box of shells Philipe had given him, and he'd filled the .44 from his belt, habitually leaving the chamber beneath the hammer empty. Now he opened the Colt's loading gate, rolled the cylinder until the empty chamber showed in the gate, and thumbed in a brass-jacketed round.

Flicking the gate closed, he spun the cylinder, vaguely enjoying the solid clicks of the well-tuned weapon, and dropped it back into its holster. Then he gave the two lead ropes a tug, ground his heels into the flanks of the well-rested roan, and loped deeper into the forbidding hills.

It was mid-afternoon before he managed to cut his own tracks from his first foray here and follow them to the base of the plateau on which he'd last seen Tremaine and Hall. Halting the horses in a brushy depression, he dismounted, grabbed his field glasses from his saddlebags, walked a ways up the gradual grade, and crouched in the shade of a black boulder.

There was little chance the desperadoes would still have his two partners pinned down behind the crag cresting the plateau, but he decided he'd better eat the apple one slow, cautious bite at a time out here. He had no idea what he'd run into.

When he'd glassed the low, jagged rock bench running from north to south across the middle of the plateau, at its peak, and seen nothing but the bench itself—and heard nothing but the breeze—he mounted up again and, leading the two spare horses, headed slowly up the grade. He hugged a shallow draw on the plateau's far left side, holding the two lead ropes in one hand while holding his own reins and his Winchester in the other.

He rode with all his senses alert, shuttling his glance in all directions. It was eerie up here. Like a graveyard on Halloween, or a gallows the morning following a hanging.

Before Longarm reached the bench, the smell of rotting flesh assaulted his nostrils. The strong, sweet fetor made him wrinkle his nose and squint his eyes. It was a stench that he'd smelled many times, but one he'd never gotten used to the way some men did—men like hide hunters he'd known.

Dread nipped at his heart. But just as he reached the bench and quickly swept the area where he'd left Hall and Tremaine, and saw no sign of them—no rotting human bodies, at least—he remembered Hall's horse. He shuttled his glance down the gradual slope on the other side of the bench.

Sure enough, the horse was there. Someone had stripped the tack from it, leaving only Hall's soogan, which lay partly unrolled in the sage and scrub beside the sprawled carcass. The horse itself was a hideous vision of bloated and rotting flesh.

Obviously, coyotes or bobcats had found the carrion, and as was nature's way, they'd begun devouring the dead creature ass-first, which was the fastest way to the delectable meat inside. The hindquarters were all but gone, and much of the backbone, tufted with dried red flesh and small patches of hide, lay exposed.

The scavengers would likely be back tonight to finish their well-seasoned meal.

Taking small breaths to keep from gagging on the eye-watering stench, Longarm took a long, careful look around. No sign of either of the two men he'd left here. Plenty of overlaid tracks—too many to get any idea of what might have happened after Longarm had ridden out under cover of darkness, or of where Hall and Tremaine had gone.

Finished looking closely around the bench, he rode up to the plateau's middle, and took another look from there. When he'd found no bodies lying anywhere along the battleground's perimeter, and no clear sign to follow—either tracks or blood—he heeled the roan through a gap in the bench wall and down the plateau's gradual slope, past where the rustlers had holed up a week ago, and back toward the canyon where Longarm had first encountered Tremaine and his captors.

In the intersecting washes down which Longarm, Hall, and Tremaine had made their short-lived escape, Longarm dismounted, tied his three horses in some well-concealed shrubs, and scouted the area on foot, holding his rifle up high and ready across his chest. There were several intersecting arroyos, with many narrow creases between the steep-sided hills of black lava. It was a hard area to cover, and only after about forty-five minutes of slow walking and searching did he come upon several dry cow pies and a few tracks of shod horses. The sign was sparse and old. And the rocky terrain made it hard to spot.

An hour after leaving the horses, Longarm spied a relatively wide gap between two tall, steep lava walls, and he hadn't walked far into the gap before he saw many dried cow pies—sign that a herd had been brought through here a couple of weeks ago. There were pies of varying ages, in fact, which probably meant that herds were hazed through here every so often.

Longarm's heart quickened its pace as he continued up the side of the gap, moving slowly and keeping his head on a cautious swivel. A couple of times he stepped around coiled rattlers, and once he gave a start at a noisy kangaroo rat.

When he saw that the gap widened about fifty yards ahead, he took two more slow strides. Something moved in the corner of his left eye, and with a soft grunt, he swung toward it, extending the Winchester out and up from his right hip.

His lower jaw dropped, and he took one step back, re-coiling. "*Ah, Christ!*"

# Chapter 16

The two bodies, hanging side by side from a branch of the stout oak at the side of the wash, turned gently in the warm, languorous breeze. About all Longarm could tell about them was that one was white and one was black. They were both bloated and badly pecked by birds, so that all distinguishing features excepting the colors of their skin were horribly distorted.

Even their clothes—dusty and bloody and drawn taut over the expanded chests and bellies—were like old newspapers left a month in a mulch crib. Longarm could make out the brass buttons on Hall's black, bib-front shirt, and a small remnant of the white piping, but that was about all. The short, curly black hair on the man's head identified him best, as did that thin, sandy, blood-caked hair of Tremaine's.

Both men's necks had been stretched six inches, and their chins brushed their chests. Their swollen, purple tongues protruded bizarrely from purple lips that had, with the effects of rot, started stretching grotesquely back from their teeth. Flies buzzed around them in a feeding frenzy. Too many bullet holes to count shone in their ragged shirts. Most would have been killing shots. The men had likely been overcome by the rustlers, shot from a distance, and then again from close range.

Many, many times.

Too many to have been necessary for killing.

In his head, Longarm could hear the jubilant whoops and hollers of the killers as they fired one shot after another into the slumped corpses.

He hadn't seen any blood around the bench behind which the two men had holed up. So they must have been killed with only a few shots up there, maybe when the rustlers had sneaked around behind them, and then dragged down here, where they'd been shot several more times before being strung up as a final desecration and as a warning to any who came snooping around.

As the light breeze swirled, the smell of putridity wafted over Longarm, making his eyes burn. His guts clenched at the smell, the loss of two good men, and at his own responsibility for their deaths.

If he hadn't run into Ana Corpus and her father's gun wolves, he might have made it back to Hall and Tremaine in time to save them. The whole mess sickened him, made him burn with regret despite the fact there was really no one to blame—including Ana and the Corpus riders—but the killers themselves.

Longarm stepped back to where the smell was less strong, and dropped to a knee, holding the Winchester high and looking around. His gloved right finger was drawn taught against the trigger. After several minutes of scanning the area around him without seeing or hearing anything suspicious, or even spotting any sign that men had been here recently, he heaved himself to his feet once more and continued forward.

Longarm's brows were ridged with befuddlement as well as apprehension. Why hadn't he seen any of the cut-throats who'd killed Hall and Tremaine? This, apparently, was where they'd hazed the stolen cattle—through here and into the canyon yonder. Surely, there were pickets about as there'd been the other day.

If they were setting a trap for him, they were damn sure taking their time in springing it.

As he approached the broad canyon, the pitted volcanic ridges drawing back behind him, he stopped and took a knee again in the shade of a sprawling cottonwood. It wasn't the only tree out there. Many cottonwoods lined the broad, deep canyon—a chasm that appeared nearly a mile square and totally surrounded by ridges of saw-toothed black lava. The sage and bunch grass and even some needle grass grew thick among the cactus—amazingly thick con-sidering the dryness of this wretched country.

But then Longarm realized why there was all this growth here. The faintly salty smell of humidity touched his nos-trils. He could feel the light caress of it against his dusty, sweaty cheeks—a balm to an open sore.

The canyon was obviously fed by a spring. And a stream apparently ran along the base of the cliff walls on the can-yon's other side, nourishing those tall cottonwoods, the fluttering tips of which were burnished gold with the west-falling light.

Just as Longarm sensed water, he could smell fresh cow shit, as well. It had a sagey, sunburnt tang to it. But as he ran his eyes back and forth across the canyon's broad meadow, carpeted in wind-buffeted grass and sage, with here and there a black boulder tumbled from the ridges above, he spotted not a single cow.

He glanced carefully around and behind him. Satisfied

he was alone, he straightened and strode into the canyon, kicking at stones and cropped clumps of grass and both old and relatively fresh cow pies. There was horse shit, as well. Longarm picked up one such apple, squeezed it, and smelled it.

Still green. Soft inside. It had probably been dropped two, no more than three, days ago.

The lawman's pulse quickened. The rustlers must have moved the cows soon after the shoot-out, soon after they'd realized one of their three quarries had slipped out of their gauntlet. Confident that he was alone here, Longarm quickened his pace as he searched for the trail over which the rustlers had hazed the cattle out of the canyon. The wash that Longarm had taken into the canyon had been used in the past, but it hadn't been used recently.

It sure as hell wasn't the portal through which the rustlers had absconded with the stolen beef.

He stumbled around for fifteen minutes, trying to get some sense of the direction the rustlers and rustled beef had headed, but quickly realized that the canyon was too damn large, with too many possible escape routes hidden by the trees lining it, to continue on foot.

Wheeling, he shouldered his rifle and strode quickly back the way he'd come, heading for the horses. It was tough walking on the rock-strewn wash, but his chiseled features were set severely, impatiently, his eyes hooded with purpose. The sun was falling fast, and he wanted to get on the rustlers' trail before dark. Likely he wouldn't be able to run them down before sunset, but at least finding the trail this afternoon would save valuable time tomorrow.

He was glad he had two spare horses. He could ride hard tomorrow, switching horses every couple of hours, always keeping at least one fresh.

What he'd do when he caught up to the rustlers, he had no idea. He needed help, but with his partners hanging from the oak, he wasn't going to get it. That was all right. He'd been outnumbered before.

He'd just have to get creative.

So intent was Longarm on getting back to the horses that he was unprepared for what he saw when he walked out of the wash—two men walking toward him, both wearing steeple-crowned sombreros and deerskin charro jackets.

And both holding old-model Colt pistols out before them. One grinning. The other—a bearded giant with a small blue cross tattooed into his right cheek—smiling mildly.

Longarm started to bring the Winchester down from his shoulder, and froze.

"I would not do that if I were you, señor," advised the man to the right of the bearded giant—a lean hombre with two short, dark red braids hanging down over his ears. He had a silver eyetooth, and a hide makings sack drooped down over the handle of another Colt in a shoulder rig.

His eyes flicked over Longarm's right shoulder.

"You might have slipped away the other night," he said, the silver tooth flashing dully, "but you are surrounded now. The light is good, and the range is close."

Longarm glanced over his shoulder. Another Mexican was moving up behind him—a little man with a face scarred from many knife fights. A white skunk streak ran through the long, coal-black hair tumbling over his left shoulder. His thick, savage lips were bunched, and his tiny pig eyes were narrowed.

"How would you like to join your friends, uh, hombre?" he grunted, tossing his head down toward the mouth of the wash where Hall and Tremaine dangled from the oak.

Crouching over the big, ivory-handled pistol in his hand, he closed quickly on Longarm, holding his free hand out as though for balance.

Lightning cracked in Longarm's head. It was a pre-death knell delivered as a warning by the god or gods who looked after fool lawmen. The only way he could prevent the real thing was to take a chance and act fast—faster than his assailants were expecting.

To that end, he let go the rifle on his shoulder. The Winchester hadn't hit the ground before he wheeled, reached across his belly, slipped his Colt from its cross-draw holster, and fired twice from his right hip.

*Pow! K-Pow!*

The little, ugly man had just started raising his ivory-handled revolver toward Longarm's head when both the lawman's slugs stopped him in mid-stride as they tore through his black, bullhide vest. The man hadn't even started stumbling backward before Longarm wheeled once more, a crouching blur of motion, and extended his smoking Colt toward the big giant.

The giant's brain hadn't yet comprehended what had happened, for Longarm had moved faster than double-geared lightning, and the man's gray-brown eyes were just snapping wide when the lawman's Colt bucked again, then once more as it slid to the man with the twin hair braids, whose own brain, apparently, hadn't worked any faster than the giant's.

As both stumbled straight back, cursing loudly in Spanish, Longarm shot them each again for good measure, then swung back to the ugly little man who'd just then dropped to both knees and popped a pill into the dirt about three inches in front of his groin. As his gun was still in his hand and he was glaring at Longarm while trying to raise the weapon, Longarm took hasty aim, and fired once more.

The .44 round drilled a neat hole just above the man's right brow, jerking his head straight back on his shoulders. He spread his arms, dropped his gun, and sank straight back on his heels, where he flopped around, gurgling, as he died.

Longarm stepped back, slowly sliding his gun back and forth between the ugly man and the other two. He'd made his decision to go for the kill so quickly, and had moved with such speed, that his heart was only now beginning to quicken. Then it began to slow again, and he'd just started to lower the smoking Colt, when a clack sounded behind him.

He spun, raising the Colt again, and dropping one knee nearly to the ground as he took quick aim at the figure thirty feet ahead of him, leading a tall, dun mare. Longarm set his sights on the short man's tan forehead, just beneath his slightly down-canted, brown hat brim, then snapped the barrel up as Ana Corpus's eyes snapped wide. She gasped and grabbed the wooden bead attached to her hat's chin thong.

Longarm froze with the Colt's barrel raised skyward, and his chiseled features hardened into miniature mesas. "That's a good way to never see womanhood, girl!"

As she stood in front of her horse in a narrow, intersecting feeder wash, Ana's eyes shifted from Longarm to the men slumped behind him. Then she returned her gaze to Longarm. "Are they dead?"

Longarm straightened and flicked open the Colt's loading gate. "They ain't resting. What the hell're you doing out here?"

"I followed you." Ana started forward, leading the horse, which flicked its ears nervously at the smell of death and cordite.

"Had a feelin' you did," Longarm growled as he plucked

the spent casings from the Colt's cylinder and looked around for more rustlers. "Where in the hell would you get such a notion?"

"I saw them on your trail." Anna stood over the dead, ugly little gent, looking down at the body with a bland expression. "If I could have got to you first, I could have warned you. Did you find your friends?"

Longarm nodded and scowled angrily at the dead cutthroats. "I found 'em all right. Hangin' from a tree yonder. Shot up like target cans."

Ana winced and turned away. "I'm sorry."

"That don't explain why you're here."

She turned back to him sharply. "Obviously, you need someone to watch your back."

"I did all right." Longarm chuffed, spinning his Colt's cylinder and dropping the piece into its holster. "And I reckon we could all use someone to watch our backs, but most of the time it don't work out that way. I get along just fine without it." His brows were hooded with anger as he set his fists on his hips. "Your father know you're here?"

Ana had picked up the dead little man's gun and was hefting it in her hand. With a scowl, she gave it a half-hearted sling down the wash and started going through the pockets of his bullhide vest. "Pa-Pa went to Claireville for a few days, to meet with cattle buyers. He is thinking of selling his herd before Pleasant Valley burns us out."

"He doesn't have a whole lot of confidence in me, does he?"

Ana was scrutinizing the few coins she'd pulled out of the dead man's pockets. Blowing grit from the glinting silver and gold in her palm, she said, "I decided to trail you. figured you would need help—one man against many." She looked around at the dead men, then regarded Longarm

with admiration in her lustrous brown eyes. "You are fast
with a pistol, Custis. I have seen none faster, and Pa-Pa has
hired some fast pistoleros over the years. But two sets of
eyes are better than one when it comes to tracking, no?"

"No," Longarm said as he wheeled and, kicking a rock
with annoyance, stomped off toward the horses. He didn't
need the help of a damn girl. She'd only get in his way, and
he'd have to worry about her when he should be concentrat-
ing solely on the men he was tracking.

He tried to put her out of his mind, but when he'd
reached his three horses, mounted the roan, and begun riding down the wash toward the canyon, she was sitting her
dun near the three dead men bleeding onto the rocks and
bleached sand.

He groaned and opened his mouth to reprimand her once
more, but she cut him off. "Look, I have nothing else to do.
And last night means something to me. I will not lie and say
it was my first time or even my second. But it was . . . special, and not just because we fucked good together. But just
because it was special. And since I can help you, and since
there is no one else around to help, I wish to help."

Her eyes narrowing, she set her long, hard jaws and
pursed her dark pink lips. "I am not going back to the
ranch, so stop being a *pendejo* and let me ride along with
you! My skulking along behind like a lone coyote will do
neither of us any good."

Longarm heaved a weary sigh, glanced at the quickly
falling sun, then heeled the roan around the dead men, jerking the other two horses along behind him. "Well, come on
then. No point in burnin' up good daylight with a bunch of
pointless palaver!"

Riding back toward the verdant canyon, he swung clear
of Hall and Tremaine. He'd fetch their bodies later and re-

turn them to their homes for proper burial. In the meantime it was more important to find the men who killed them than to tend to two dead bodies desecrated nearly beyond recognition.

When Longarm and Ana reached the mouth of the broad canyon, Longarm turned to the girl, whose dun had been stepping along smartly beside him. "You ever seen this place before?"

She was looking around, holding up a gloved hand to shield her eyes from the sun cresting the canyon walls on their left. "*Dios mío*. No. There must be water here. I didn't think there was any water in the lava bluffs."

"I reckon that's why this was a pretty smart place for them long-loopers to hold a stolen herd while they added to it a little bit at a time. Good place to fatten the herd for the long trail, too."

"The long trail to where?"

"That's what we're gonna find out. Sometime in the past coupla days after I, Hall, and Tremaine rode up on 'em, they lit a shuck out of here." Longarm looked around, then pointed to the left. "You ride along the west side of the canyon. Keep your eyes skinned for another way out of here besides the wash behind us. They brought plenty of cows in this way, but they've taken them out some other. If you see anything, trigger a shot. If I see anything, I'll do likewise."

Ana narrowed an eye at him. "You're not trying to lose me, are you?"

"Nah." Longarm spared a grin. "I reckon now that you're here I might as well put you to work."

# Chapter 17

Longarm did indeed put Ana to work scouting for the route the rustlers took out of the canyon, but it was Longarm himself who spotted the brush-choked notch in the canyon's northeast ridge through which a good-sized herd of cattle had recently been hazed. The ground all around the notch's mouth, on the other side of the narrow stream running through the cottonwoods, was littered with cow shit, horse shit, and countless overlaid cloven-hoof tracks.

Longarm glanced through the darkening cottonwoods and across the canyon, toward where Ana was scouting the canyon's far side. His gaze sharpened with cunning.

Should he leave her?

It would be a damn dirty trick after promising to take her along, but he didn't want to get her killed, either.

Ah, hell. She'd just track him down and give him an earful. Texas was sure filled with headstrong girls.

He triggered a shot into the air without worrying who heard it. Likely, only the rustlers had occupied the canyon for some time, and, unfortunately, they were probably well out of hearing.

A couple of minutes after his shot had finished echoing around the canyon, and as he was topping off his two canteens at the gurgling stream, Longarm saw the girl galloping toward him across the canyon floor—a brown speck growing gradually larger until she and the dun trotted through the cottonwoods, splashed across the stream, and drew up beside Longarm, all four horses nickering greetings to one another.

Ana's thick hair jostled across her shoulders, and her ample breasts pushed out from behind her long-sleeved white blouse trimmed with red piping. The blouse contrasted the honey-tan of her skin and the dark brown of her hair.

Ana gave Longarm a cockeyed smile, as though she knew that he'd been considering leaving her, and then they put their horses into the rocky notch, following the well-trampled path between more high, pitted, black ridges.

"Dark soon," Longarm said as the horses clomped over the rubble-strewn wash. "I don't want to try to follow the trail at night and risk losing it. We'll hole up in an hour and pull out first thing in the morning."

They each rode silently.

The trail of such a large herd wasn't hard to follow, so Longarm kept his eyes skinned on the ridges rising and falling on either side of the wash. The last thing he wanted was to ride into an ambush. This pack of curly wolves might very well have only started moving the herd and laid up a little ways from the main canyon to lure him into a trap, to get shed at the outset of their journey of any and all shadowers.

Such an ambush wasn't likely, but Longarm had learned in his years of manhunting that expecting the unlikely was the best way to live to a ripe old retirement age.

Occasionally his glance wandered down the ridges to Ana riding several yards to his right and trailing one of the two spare horses. He liked the way she rode—easy and light in the saddle, arms up and elbows close to her sides, guiding the horse with small nudges from her knees as well as her heels, and with occasional clucks and whispered phrases. She cast her gaze all around, too, not just on the canyon floor. She knew it was a dangerous mission that she and Longarm were on, and all her senses were attuned to her surroundings.

A tough one, this girl. And she looked like she'd been born in that saddle. Longarm didn't doubt that she'd raised the dun mare from a foal, and gentled and trained the mount herself. Girl and horse moved as one.

The wash twisted along its path toward a low rise of cone-topped mountains that the falling sun burnished to the color of old pennies. When the mountains turned to dark silhouettes humped against the green, ever-darkening sky, the rustlers' trail followed the wash into a broad *malpais* that stretched away to a gap between what appeared to be two separate eastern ranges.

Here, where there was no natural course to follow, it would be too damn easy to lose the trail. Longarm angled the roan toward a clump of mesquites backed by a low, chalky shelf. It was about the only cover he could see out here on this ancient lake bed, where there was nothing but rocks and cactus for miles all around.

"We'll stop there," he said.

"How's your head?"

"Huh?" Longarm looked at Ana, who regarded him side-long, concern in her gaze. "Oh, I reckon it's all right."

So intent had he been on the killers' trail that he hadn't paid much attention to his aches and pains. But the girl's question made him aware of a bone-deep fatigue. He'd be glad to hit the bedroll and to pull his hat down over his eyes.

When they'd tended the horses and picketed them close, in what little grass grew along the base of the small, chalky shelf, Ana gathered mesquite branches and built a fire. Longarm made coffee. He'd have been content with only jerky for supper, but Ana had packed a couple of potatoes and dried antelope, and cooked up a stew of sorts in a frying pan. She'd brought biscuits, as well, and she heated those on a rock near the small, crackling flames.

It wasn't quite good dark, with the coyotes calling from the far mountains, before Longarm tossed his coffee dregs over his shoulder, leaned back against his saddle, and kicked out of his boots. He pulled his hat brim over his eyes.

"Thanks for supper, girl. Not bad vittles for out here on this boil on Old Scratch's ass. Now . . ." His voice grew thick as sleep overwhelmed him. "I reckon I'll just . . . sorta . . ."

He heard his words trail off, replaced by a clipped, throaty snore. A short time later, something damp touched his cheek, and he snapped his eyes open.

"Shh," Ana said. She was dabbing at his left cheek with a wet bandana. "I am just cleaning this cut. It came open. Shh, Custis. Go back to sleep."

He grumbled, smacked his lips, and did as he was told.

He got up during the night to pee and found her lying on her bedroll spread beside his. She lay curled on her side, turned away from him, with her butt rammed up against his leg. Her rump was warm, intoxicating as a shot of Maryland rye. When he'd stumbled away in his socks, maneuvering by starlight, and drained his bladder on a dead greasewood shrub, he returned to his bedroll.

Now Ana lay facing his blankets, resting her cheek on her hands. Her top blanket was pulled down below her shoulders.

She'd unbuttoned her blouse a ways, and her dark cleavage bubbled out of the gap, restrained by only a thin, lace-edged camisole. Longarm snorted, lay down, turned toward her, and ran his right index finger lightly across her left nipple peeking out of the open shirt and low chemise. She muttered something unintelligible, then rolled over, kicked, squirmed, and began snoring softly.

Longarm chuckled. Despite the old pull in his pants, he was glad she hadn't responded to his lascivious caress. She was a tasty little thing, nicely curved and rounded, and despite his minor miseries, he would have done the old mattress dance with her. But he needed his sleep more than he needed a romp.

He lay back, noted a single falling star sparking in the high-up heavens, and pulled his hat down over his eyes.

Instantly, he slept.


Longarm and Ana were on the rustlers' trail at first light, riding hard and switching horses every hour, stopping only to rest the mounts and give them water, maybe a handful of oats from their saddlebags.

They rode between the two black ranges and swerved south.

"Mexico," Longarm muttered. "I figured."

"What?"

"They're headed for Mexico," Longarm said, his voice vibrating with the choppy trot of his second horse. "But they're ranging wide of Claireville and most likely any towns between here and the border."

"The border is a three-day ride from here," Ana said.

Longarm scrubbed the sweat dripping down his face with his bandana. "Want to head home?"

"No," she shot out. "I was just pointing out it could be a long ride. Me—I am ready for anything. You, on the other hand, have had a tumble, in case you don't remember. And that cheek has opened up again."

"A recent tumble and winging delivered by you and your cutthroats!" Longarm said with a laugh, swiping his bandana across the bleeding cut on his cheek.

Ana hiked a shoulder, and her mouth quirked with a grin. "You are a suspicious character, Longarm. You're just lucky I spotted your badge, or you'd be feeding the desert pumas." A shadow swept her features, and her dark brows wrinkled. "I am just sorry to have caused the deaths of two innocent men."

"Wasn't your fault," Longarm said. "You were just protecting your range. It's Woolyard's fault as much as yours or mine. The rustlers killed Hall and Tremaine, and I aim to make them . . ."

He'd heard something. He stared straight ahead, frowning.

"What is it?"

"Hear that?"

"What?"

"Listen."

Nothing for a second. Then a cow's moo sounded in the far distance, barely audible against the softly sighing breeze.

"*Mierda*," Ana whispered.

Longarm stood up tall in his stirrups, staring over the sparse greasewood that covered the low hogbacks before him. "Could be Pleasant Valley cows," he said, frowning into the sun-blistered distance but seeing nothing except more of the same olive-colored forage and low, rocky hills.

"Not this late in the year." Ana, too, tried to get a look into the far distance, turning her head this way and that, kicking her stirrups out like wings. "This late in the year, Pleasant Valley brings their herds closer to the main range. Pa-Pa's men are bringing our herds up from the southwest. No one else has cows out here—this far east." Her voice dropped a couple octaves. "Woolyard ran the 'nesters,' as he calls them, out of this part of the range."

The intermittent mooing continued, some fainter than the rest. The sounds seemed to be coming from ahead and south.

Longarm touched his heels to the piebald's flanks and jerked the roan's lead line, continuing forward at a fast, deliberate walk. It wasn't long before he and Ana crested a camelback and saw, spread out before them, across a broad, shallow valley lined with cottonwoods at the far edge, a good-sized herd of cattle. From this distance they looked like pepper dusting a tabletop, but Longarm could tell they were a white-faced mix of prime beef.

Pleasant Valley beef.

He and Ana didn't linger atop the hogback, where they were outlined against the sky behind them, but gigged their horses into the crease between that hill and the next. Longarm dismounted quickly, dropping the piebald's reins—the Corpus horses were well trained and easily ground-tied—and jogged back to dig his field glasses out of his saddlebags draped across the roan's back.

He scrambled up the next hill, Ana close on his heels, and dropped to his knees just below the crest. Raising the field glasses so he could see just over the weed-tufted lip, he adjusted the focus until he'd brought the herd up close enough that he could make out individual features as well as the small, adobe-brick cabin that stood with a pole corral and what appeared to be a dilapidated barn off to the right. The cabin was a dugout protruding from the side of a low bluff.

Longarm swept the glasses over the cattle once more. Here and there, men on horseback rode at the herd's perimeters. Bringing the glasses back to the disheveled ranchstead, Longarm saw that there were half a dozen horses in the pole corral. As many saddles were draped over the top of the corral—mostly heavy rigs with big, Texas-style horns.

Three or four men milled in front of the cabin. Longarm spotted a couple of wagon wheel sombreros amid the group, and several brightly colored bandanas. All the men were dressed in denim and leather, and revolvers jutted from holsters on their hips or thighs. A couple of rifles leaned against benches fronting the cabin.

"Is it them?" Ana asked.

Longarm tried to focus on one cow, but he was too far away to see the brand on its flank. "Can't tell. But if you're right and no one else has cows out here, who else could it be?"

"I am usually right," Ana said without irony, lying belly down as she stretched her gaze over the top of the bluff. "And as you say, who else would it be?"

Longarm snorted. Ana grabbed the glasses away from him. He snorted again at the girl's pluck, then scooted a ways farther down the bluff and dug a cheroot from his shirt pocket. He bit off the end and fished a lucifer from the same pocket in which he kept his dwindling supply of three-for-a-nickel cigars.

Nothing like a smoke to help him think.

As he fired the match on his shell belt, Ana lowered the glasses and scooted down the bluff on her belly until she was beside Longarm. She glanced at him darkly and shook her head. It wasn't hard to tell what she was thinking.

One lawman and a local ranch girl against that crew of rustlers? The curly wolves had killed two men as easily as kicking dog dung off a bunkhouse porch. They wouldn't bat an eye at killing one more and a girl.

"Yeah, I know," Longarm replied to her silent question. "What I wanna know is why'd they stop so soon? Maybe they ain't takin' 'em to Mexico after all. But where?"

"Maybe you better ride back to Claireville and get the sheriff to help you. Or telegraph someone for help."

Longarm took a deep-lunged drag off the cigar and rested an arm on an upraised knee. "The rustlers would likely be gone by the time I got back."

She gave him a tough, determined look. "So what are we going to do?"

"*We're* not gonna do *nothin'*! *I'm* gonna wait for dark, and then *I'm* gonna sneak in close to the cabin and see what I'm up against. Then I'm gonna figure a way of takin' that crew down without getting plucked, dressed, and greased for the pan."

"What about me?" she snapped, indignant.

"You're gonna stay right here with the horses."

Ana crossed her arms on her breasts and sat back against the bluff, brown eyes spitting fire. "Alone, you don't have a chance!"

"You're probably right," Longarm allowed, taking another deep drag off the cheroot and looking around to make sure no pickets were out this far from the herd. "But I don't aim to get you killed, too, Ana. So you do what I say, or I'll take you over my knee."

"You would like that!" She chuffed.

Longarm ran his eyes across her angrily heaving bosom and grinned. "Yeah, I reckon I would."

# Chapter 18

"You stay, ya here?" Longarm said, narrowing a severe eye at Ana.

It was good dark. Stars flashed and sparkled. The cattle were lowing and someone was strumming a guitar near the cabin. Occasional whoops of jovial laughter rose.

"I hear," the girl said with another chuff. She sank back against the bluff again, eyes hooded with anger. "And what am I supposed to do while you are gone?"

"Stay with the horses, keep 'em quiet. If there's shooting, make sure they don't scare and run." Longarm touched his forefinger to his hat brim as he rose and turned away. "I'll be back."

"If you're not?"

"Like I told you, damnit." He stopped and glanced back at her. "Give me two hours. If I'm not back by then—or if you hear men heading this way *before* then—you step into your saddle and hightail it back to Wolf Creek!"

"And *leave* you?"

The girl's incredulous hiss was almost inaudible behind Longarm as he made his way down to the base of the butte and started tramping around it, heading in the general direction of the herd. He held his borrowed rifle in his right hand, and he kept his hat brim low so the starlight wouldn't reflect off his eyes and cheekbones. He'd already removed the bandage from around his head, as the white fabric would stand out like a target. The flaps of his black frock covered his shell belt.

He kept his head down as he made his way toward the lowing cattle, the Mexican strains of the guitar, and the murmur of distant voices. Halfway between his starting point and the cabin he had to hole up behind a boulder as a picket rider clomped past him—a tall, lean gent in a palm-leaf sombrero and pinto vest, with ornately stitched *tapaderos* over his stirrups. The Mexican-style stirrup covers marked him as a brush rider—probaby a long-looping bandito from the Texas *brasada*. He must have been smoking a quirley hidden in his cupped palm; Longarm couldn't see the glow but he could smell the harsh tobacco on the mild, still night air.

Fifteen minutes after the picket rider had hoofed on past him, humming softly to the guitar chords, Longarm crawled the last thirty yards to a low wash running at an angle off the cabin's northeast corner. The cabin was a long stone's throw from the wash, but with the field glasses, which he'd carried strapped to his belt, he figured to get a close-up look at how many cutthroats he was up against, and how well-armed they were.

He hunkered down beneath an ironwood branch that was only about three feet off the ground, at the gully's edge. Making sure there were no snakes or poisonous spiders about, he dropped to his elbows in the wiry brush between two rocks and raised the glasses. The rustlers—if that's who this bunch was—had a big bonfire burning about twenty yards out from the cabin.

What appeared a quarter side of beef was roasting on a spit over the fire, and a short, paunchy man in silver-tipped boots was turning it slowly with a long-handled crank while taking frequent sips from a bottle so clear that the fire shone brightly through it, as though liquid gold were inside.

Longarm draped the ends of his hands over the binocular lenses, so they wouldn't reflect the firelight. Three Mexicans, including the cook, stood around the fire, drinking, while a fourth sat in a backless chair a ways out from the cabin's dilapidated porch, strumming the guitar. He was a burly gent with a thick beard, and he wore three pistols on his person, with a hide-wrapped knife handle jutting from the well of his right boot.

Behind him, shadows moved in the lighted cabin window and open doorway, and voices sounded from in there, as well. Two men, it sounded like, were speaking English, but above the outside conversation and guitar Longarm couldn't hear what the men inside were saying.

He'd slid the glasses toward where the herd grazed left of the cabin, to see if any other men were close, when he glimpsed a figure moving toward the fire from the corral beyond it. Tightening his hands around the ends of the glasses, he trained them on the newcomer.

His furrowed brows nudged the glasses slightly when a girl's voice said sharply, "Montana! Why aren't you catching the drippings like I instructed?"

At the same time, Longarm saw long, honey-blond hair dancing on the newcomer's slender shoulders as she marched toward the man swilling tequila and turning the beef. A long, doeskin riding skirt buffeted against her long legs, and a wide black belt encircled her narrow waist below the swollen mounds of her breasts pushing out from behind a pale blue, puffy-sleeved blouse.

The guitar strummer and the other men laughed as the cook turned to the girl, spread his arms, and lifted his shoulders.

"I don know," he said in a thick Mexican accent, drunkenly slurring his words. He canted his head toward the smoking, sizzling beef suspended above the leaping flames and glowing coals. "You wanna cook the fucking beef, Señorita Woolyard, you can cook it. But that means you got to crank it, and she's a *heavy* fuckin' heifer!"

The cook and the other Mexicans laughed heartily, the guitar player raking his hand across the strings raucously and nearly falling off his chair.

Verna's lower jaw dropped, and in the fire's glow Longarm saw her eyes widen and her jaws harden, her fists clench at her sides. She opened her mouth to put the cook in his place, but before she could get the words out, a familiar, heavily Scottish-accented voice boomed from the cabin: "Verna, what have I told you about fraternizing with my . . . associates?"

Longarm slid the glasses toward the cabin door. A tall, stooped figure stood there, supported by crutches. He was mostly silhouetted by the light behind him, but the amber firelight flickered over thick, curly, iron-gray hair and muttonchop whiskers. Longarm was still trying to wrap his mind around the fact that Verna Woolyard was out here, and the added fact that her father was out here, as well, was too much to take in all at once.

"Papa, this behemoth is too drunk to cook!"

"Verna, get in here!" Woolyard ordered. "What the hell are you doin' traipsin' around out there, anyways, ya damn loony girl?"

"I was checking my horse," Verna said, slouching toward the cabin but raking her haughty gaze over the snickering Mexicans behind her. "I was making sure the scrub mounts of your associates weren't taking apple-sized bites out of Indigo's hide!"

As the girl brushed past her father, disappearing into the cabin, Woolyard said, "Garza, keep your men on a short leash, goddamnit! My daughter isn't one of your border *putas*, understand? You're to treat her like a lady."

One of the men standing on the far side of the fire—a slender gent with the high, clean-shaven cheeks of an Indian and short, black hair beneath his black Stetson, merely grinned at Woolyard scowling from the door. The firelight flashed on his large, white teeth.

Woolyard scoffed. As he turned back into the cabin, hobbling on his crutches, Longarm could barely hear him say, "No, you wouldn't understand, would you?"

Then he was gone, and the thumps of his crutches on a hard-packed earthen floor dwindled.

The Mexicans chuckled and shared snide glances. The guitar player began strumming again, and sang through his snickers.

Like a man waking from a bizarre dream that clung to him like cockleburs to a shaggy cur, Longarm lowered the binoculars, dropped his butt down into the wash, and rested his back against the bank.

I'll be goddamned, he thought.

As his mind spun like a roulette wheel through several possible explanations for what he'd just seen, he wondered if he'd followed the wrong herd. Maybe Woolyard was only out here with his men, several of whom were Mexican, bringing a cavvy closer to home for the oft-tumultuous Texas winter.

No.

Longarm had followed this herd from the verdant canyon in the lava bluffs.

Thumping sounds rose from the direction of the cabin, interrupting Longarm's racing thoughts. He rose and turned toward the cabin, hunkering low beneath the ironwood branch. A figure had stepped out of the cabin. Not Woolyard or Verna, but . . .

Longarm quickly raised the field glasses without bothering to shield the lenses with his hands. He adjusted the focus slightly, training the two semicircles of magnified vision on the man hobbling out of the cabin, past the guitar player, and into the yard. The man's profile was to Longarm, so all he could see was that he was an hombre of average height and build, wearing a cream Stetson with a broad brim upturned slightly at the edges. Thick, wavy dark hair curled over his ears.

What caught the brunt of Longarm's attention, however, was the man's left leg. Or lack thereof.

Sure as shit in cow country, the man was sporting a wooden peg where his left leg should have been. Slinking around behind him, from where it must have been skulking in the shadows of the cabin wall, was a mutt that looked at least half-coyote.

California Todd?

As if to answer Longarm's question, Todd sidled up to one of the men on the far side of the fire and turned his face so that Longarm could see nearly his entire, handsome, dimple-chinned visage. Todd grabbed a bottle out of the hand of one of the Mexicans on the far side of the fire from the cabin, just as the man was about to take a drink, and, chuckling, rubbed the palm of his hand over the lip.

"You boys best not get yourself too pie-eyed," the sheriff said good-naturedly, the five-pointed star on his vest flashing in the firelight. "We're gonna hit the trail early, ride till late. It's a damn long haul back to the border."

Todd sat down on a log beside the small, lean hombre whom Longarm took to be the leader of the Mexican rustlers. The two men began conversing in low tones while the guitar player continued strumming and singing softly, intimately, hunkered low over his instrument.

Todd's sharp-nosed dog had been sniffing at the roasting beef, but now as Longarm slowly lowered the binoculars, a knowing grin shaping itself on his lips and lifting the ends of his longhorn mustache—what was going on out here had suddenly dawned on him like the sun of a fresh spring morning—the dog turned abruptly toward him.

"Oh, shit," Longarm muttered as the mutt started walking, head and tail down, nose working, toward the gully in which the lawman hunkered.

When the dog was only about twenty feet away, it slowed its pace and, staring into the brush in which Longarm hunkered now even lower, began to sort of mewl and growl suspiciously.

"Damn mutt!" Longarm hissed under his breath.

"Louie!" Todd called. "What the hell you doin' over there? Be careful of them damn coyote bitches! They'll lure you off and fuck you to *death*, old son!"

The Mexicans laughed. Todd's dimple-cheeked grin slowly faded as he watched his mutt slinking low toward the brushy gully. Longarm's heart began thumping like a war drum. He was about to get rooted out of his cover by a damn dog.

Rooted out and drilled seven ways from sundown!

He crabbed back into the gully, looking around as if for somewhere to hide. But there was nowhere to hide from a damn dog with a foreign scent in its sniffer. As he pulled his head down behind the gully's lip, he reached for his gun. He might have to shoot it out right here and now, starting with the corrupt, peg-legged sheriff's snoopy dog.

"Louie, what the hell you see over there?" Behind the fast-approaching, growling mutt, California Todd heaved himself to his feet, drawing his long-barreled Colt from the holster thonged low on his right thigh. "Fellas," he said to the men around him, "we best check this out."

"Ah, Christ," Longarm growled, sliding his own Colt from its holster and gritting his teeth as the Mexicans staggered to their feet and reached for their sidearms.

*Here we go!*

# Chapter 19

Longarm backed away from the wash's low bank, his cocked revolver in one hand, his rifle and field glasses in the other. The dog was coming at him, hackles raised, fangs chopping, threatening mewls bubbling up from deep in its scrawny chest.

Longarm aimed and tightened his trigger finger. Suddenly, he relaxed it.

The god that watches over dogs and fools deposited a memory into his consciousness, and as his eyes snapped wide, he lowered the Colt slightly, dropped the rifle and glasses, and reached into his coat pocket. He'd shoved a couple of Ana's biscuits, with cooked jerky laid between the gravy-basted halves, into his left pocket a few hours ago, to nibble when he felt he needed nourishment.

Behind the dog's low-slung head and attack-tense body, California Todd and his Mexican cohorts moved toward the wash, guns out, Todd skip-hopping on his peg leg while expertly maintaining his balance.

"What is it, Louie?" the sheriff called. "Go on after it . . . long as it ain't no puma or such!"

"Hey, Louie," Longarm hissed, holding out one of the three biscuits. "How 'bout a treat for your mangy ass?"

Instantly, the mewling died in the cur's throat, its pointy ears pricked, and its snout dropped slightly toward the food. Its bushy tail gave a cautious wag.

Louie gave several sharp sniffs and whimpered.

"Go get it, Louie!" Longarm slung the biscuit up the wash.

The dog yipped loudly, leaped down the bank with a grunt and another eager bark, and sprinted up the wash.

"Git it, Louie!" Todd shouted as the Mexicans lurched into runs, leaving the hobbling Todd behind.

At the same time, Longarm grabbed his rifle and field glasses and, holstering the Colt, sprinted down the wash, in the opposite direction from the dog. When he heard his pursuers crashing through the brush behind him, he leaped up the opposite bank. He paused to toss another biscuit into the wash on the far side of the gulley, to throw the dog off his scent, then hunkered behind a scraggly cottonwood, looking into the wash.

The Mexicans were irregularly shaped silhouettes moving cautiously through the brush and into the gully, muttering among themselves. Behind them, Todd thumped along, calling softly but clearly on the still night air, "What is it? You boys see anything?"

Satisfied the men hadn't seen him, Longarm jogged up the wash, then swerved behind a low butte. He continued moving east, skirting the herd he could occasionally see between buttes off to his right. Most of the cows appeared to be bedded down for the night, though a few stood grazing. He kept his distance from the cattle, so they wouldn't give away his presence like old Louie had done.

Working his way east along the edge of the herd, he

dropped to a knee now and then and listened above the rasps of his own labored breaths, hearing nothing to indicate that either the dog or the men were shadowing him. He continued eastward until he'd reached what appeared to be the far eastern edge of the herd. Then, looking and listening, knowing there would be nighthawks out here, keeping a close eye on the herd, he hoofed it south, a course of action cementing itself in his mind.

Twice he spied a horseback rider amid the idle cattle. One man sat his horse near the edge of the herd. He appeared to be a white man, judging by his gringo-looking attire, but Longarm couldn't be sure in the darkness. Another man rode slowly amid the cows, humming softly as though to keep the cattle calm. This hombre, too, was too far away for Longarm to tell if he was Mex or gringo, but he appeared to wear a low-crowned cream hat.

Longarm wasn't sure why that mattered, but he was still half-consciously trying to get a total understanding of Woolyard's doings.

He moved slowly to the crest of a low hill, stopped, and scrambled a few feet back from the top. A tingling in his veins told him he'd found what he'd been looking for.

About fifty yards from the base of the hill he was on, a low coffee fire glowed amid a sparse scattering of mesquites and greasewood shrubs. Longarm bit his lip and opened and closed his hand on his borrowed rifle as he stared through the trees.

He'd figured there would be another camp out here, on the other side of the herd, to prevent anyone from closing on the herd from the east. Along with the guards would be the guards' horses.

He needed a horse. And he needed one on this side of the herd.

Longarm couldn't see much but the fire's dull, amber glow and the silhouetted branches, and he wasn't going to see anything more until he got closer.

Dropping back down the hill, he ran around the side of it, scrambled to the edge of the trees, and got down and crawled on all fours toward the camp. Twenty feet from the fire, he stopped his painstakingly slow crawl and peered over the top of a low rock.

Two men were hunkered down around the fire, drinking coffee. One was on one knee, laying out a game of solitaire in the dirt in front of his left boot. The other lay back against his saddle, darning a filthy sock and squinting at his effort. Both were *norteamericanos*, the one playing solitaire a good ten years younger than the other. The sock mender had a Henry rifle leaning against his saddle, within easy reach.

But he had the sock pulled down over his left hand, and he held the thread and needle in his right.

Longarm gave a slight, self-satisfied smile.

He climbed to a knee, thumbing his Winchester's hammer back with a resolute click. He said just loudly enough for the two men around the fire to hear him: "One move and you're both deader'n last year's Thanksgiving turkey."

Both men jerked with starts and whipped their gazes toward Longarm. The solitaire player—a kid with thick blond curls tumbling down from his brown slouch hat—closed his fingers over the grip of a pistol angled over his belly.

The kid's blue eyes flashed cunningly in the firelight.

"Don't do it," Longarm warned, pressing the rifle's stock against his jaw and drawing a bead on the kid's head, just below his hat brim. The kid kept his hand on his pistol grip.

Longarm glanced at the sock mender. The man had slipped the sock halfway up his hand, regarding Longarm with a look similar to the kid's. Longarm could almost hear their hearts thudding in their chests.

"Don't do it, you stupid bastards," Longarm barked. "I got you dead to goddamn rights!"

But he hadn't finished his plea before the kid jerked around toward him, bringing up a pearl-gripped Remington so quickly that he nearly got the damn thing leveled on Longarm before Longarm squeezed the Winchester's trigger.

The kid said, "Oh!" and flew back in the dirt with a thud.

Longarm ejected the spent shell over his shoulder, seated a fresh one in the Winchester's chamber, and slid the barrel toward the sock mender. This man, too, was fast.

But not fast enough.

Just as he whipped up his Henry rifle, Longarm drilled a .44 round through his throat. The man gave a grotesque, gurgling scream as he flew back over his saddle, triggering his Henry into the air above his head. The bullet clipped a branch from a tall mesquite, and the branch tumbled straight down to the ground, landing with a crunching thud across the sock mender's kicking feet.

Longarm lunged forward, glanced at the kid, who lay still, then at the sock mender, who was rolling in a fit of unbearable pain, closing one hand over his bloody throat while trying to snake a long-barreled Smith & Wesson out of a shoulder holster.

"Damn fool," Longarm grated out, and put the man out of his misery with a heart shot.

When the echo of the shot had died, Longarm ejected the spent shell, but before seating a fresh one in the chamber, he cocked his head to listen. In the distance, from the direction of the heard, a man shouted. Then another. The cattle were mooing, and judging by the low hoof thuds, the herd was up and moving around, unsettled by the gunshots.

Faster thuds rose then, as well, growing quickly louder. Bridle chains rattled. One of the nighthawks was riding fast toward Longarm.

Longarm rammed a shell into the Winchester's chamber, then quickly thumbed fresh ones from his cartridge belt into the rifle's receiver. He grabbed the dead sock mender's saddle and blanket, and stumbled away from the fire, looking for the dead men's horses. It didn't take him long to find the mounts, as both were stomping around and nickering where they'd been tethered a ways east of the fire.

As the cattle increased their mooing and nervous milling, and the clomps of the approaching rider grew louder from the direction of the herd, Longarm leaned his rifle against a tree and went to work bridling and saddling one of the two stock ponies—a black-and-white pinto—tied to a short picket line stretched between two trees. He tightened the latigo, grabbed his rifle, and swung up into the leather.

"*Kinch!*" a voice called as brush snapped and cracked under a horse's thudding hooves. "*Mills!*"

Longarm looked back through the trees, beyond the low fire and the still forms of the two dead men. A silhouette dodged and shifted, and as Longarm reined the horse toward the fire, swerving left of it, staying within the darkness at its edge, the horseback rider edged close enough to the light that Longarm could see a tall man in a denim jacket and wide-brimmed black hat holding a rifle straight up in one hand. He was putting the horse quickly through the trees, heading toward the fire, which reflected off the breech of his Spencer repeater.

"Kinch!" he shouted, louder this time, his voice pitched

with anxiety. "Mills, goddamnit, who's shootin'? Them cows is ready to—!"

His head turned sharply toward Longarm as the lawman edged the pinto around a mesquite thicket. Longarm leveled his Winchester and rode toward the man. "Hold it there, amigo!"

Teeth flashed between the man's thin lips, and his Spencer's barrel came down. There was a ratcheting click as he thumbed the rifle's hammer back. "Hold this, you son of a bitch!"

Longarm's Winchester boomed. The rustler's Spencer thundered half a wink later, the slug tearing into the mesquite thicket flanking Longarm while the shooter himself rolled neatly off the back of his paint. The horse bucked, turned, and galloped off through the woods.

Racking a fresh round one-handed, Longarm jerked the pinto left and booted him through the trees and into the clearing. He checked the horse down, and it skitter-stepped as Longarm looked around.

Straight west, the black shapes of the cows were shifting this way and that, like separate currents in the same stream. Not one animal was still lying down, and they were all raising a plaintive, frightened cacophony. Occasionally, the quick thuds of running hooves sounded, setting an entire small group to fleeing, as well.

Beyond the dark mass of the herd, a little to the left of Longarm, the fire fronting the cabin flashed and sparked like a growing pyramid. It was hard to tell from this distance and in the darkness, but Longarm thought he saw a couple of horseback riders moving toward him through the herd, spaced about sixty yards apart.

Beneath the herd's mounting rumble, a deep voice shouted angrily.

Longarm flared his nostrils and stared toward the cabin from beneath his down-canted hat brim.

Woolyard.

"Damn fool," Longarm said, smiling. "Ain't you been around cows long enough to know it don't take all that much to make 'em stampede? In fact, I'm a mite surprised the gunfire hasn't set 'em off already. Ah, well—I bet this will!"

Grinding his heels against the pinto's flanks, he galloped toward the herd like he'd been shot out of a cannon.

# Chapter 20

Old trail salts often said that trying to stop a herd of stampeding cattle was like trying to stop a fully stoked train on the downgrade. Longarm knew that was true, because he'd seen stampedes before. Before he'd started lawdogging, in fact, he'd been around a few—and around one was where you wanted to be, as opposed to inside of one.

Inside of one, you had very little chance of ever seeing daylight again.

Now, as Longarm stormed across the broad clearing on his borrowed pinto, heading in the general direction of the cook fire and the cabin, and hazing the thundering herd along before him, he watched a couple of Woolyard's horseback riders go down hard and fast. The screams of both horses and men were shrill and clipped, drowned out by the bellowing beeves and the deafening hammering of scissoring hooves.

Woolyard was shouting near the cabin, and Longarm heard a pistol pop and saw the flash of a gun maw aimed skyward not far from the cabin's open door. The Scotsman was trying to turn the herd from the hovel. Faintly, Verna's screams rose, and then there was another familiar voice—the excited cries of California Todd. Longarm was too far away—a good two hundred yards—to see any of the three, but judging by the pitch of their shouts, they were trying to scare the cattle away from the cabin.

As Longarm stared in that direction, the fire flickered, then suddenly spread, sparks flying in all directions. More shouts rose, and then something sizzled through the air about a foot in front of Longarm's head. He swiveled his head right as a gun's pop reached his ears. A horseback rider was galloping toward him, starlight flashing off tack and weapons.

There was a small, red flash. Longarm ducked as another bullet screeched past him. Keeping the pinto heading toward the cabin, well back of the thundering herd, he swung his rifle out one-handed and squeezed the trigger.

The Winchester bucked and roared.

The rider kept coming, angling toward Longarm. His black shape was crouching low in the saddle, and as he drew within fifty yards of Longarm, he raised his own rifle with both hands, shoving the stock up against his shoulder.

Longarm straightened suddenly, hauling back on the pinto's reins. The rustler's rifle barked. A slug screamed off a rock to Longarm's left. As the pinto ground its rear hooves into the sand and gravel, skidding, Longarm took his Winchester in both hands, and aimed.

*Boom!*

The hard case's horse screamed. The man gave an indignant bellow.

His dark shape flew back against his horse's left hip and sagged toward the ground, his hat and rifle tumbling away. Only the man's head and shoulders hit the turf, however. As the horse continued on past Longarm and the nickering pinto, Longarm saw that the man's right boot had gotten caught in the stirrup.

"*Madre Mariaaaaaaaaa!*"

His wail faded as the horse dragged him on past Longarm and southward over a low hogback, the loud smacks of his back and head hitting the rocky ground dwindling quickly.

Levering a fresh cartridge into the Winchester's chamber, and making a mental note that the borrowed rifle shot a little high and right, Longarm looked around. He didn't see any more riders near him. Not living ones, at least. A couple of shapes humped on the ground ahead and left, where two nighthawks must have gotten caught inside the herd when the beeves had started to run. Far ahead and left, toward a small stand of trees, he heard a man's agonized wail, and as Longarm put the pinto forward, the wail dwindled to silence.

The black mass of the herd had pushed into the hills beyond the cabin, their bellowing growing softer but still echoing. Dust sifted in the air behind them. The ground was torn up, greasewood shrubs and small mesquites ripped out of the ground and shredded.

"Let's go," Longarm said, touching the pinto's flanks with his heels, easing the horse into a lope while he looked around cautiously for more of Woolyard's men.

Beyond the dull thuds of his own horse, an eerie silence had descended over the hillocks and hogbacks. Above, stars shimmered with a cold indifference.

The cabin was dark. The fire had gone out.

Fifty yards from the small, adobe-brick shack, Longarm checked the pinto down. He swept his gaze over the broken ground and the rocks and small hummocks behind which a gunman might be hiding. Stepping out of the saddle, he dropped the pinto's reins and moved ahead slowly, holding the rifle in both hands.

Ahead, the cabin was dark. The thickly sifting dust made it appear swathed in a fine, tan gauze.

Something moved down low against the small, black rectangle of the closed door. There was a wooden rasp, and then a ragged breath.

"Sonso' . . ." a man wheezed. "Sons o' fuckin' *bitches*!"

Longarm dropped to a knee and raised the rifle out from his shoulder, lining up the sights on the figure slumped down against the base of the cabin door. He'd thrown a hand up toward the latch, and he sort of hung there, his head down, legs curled beneath him.

Longarm thumbed the Winchester's hammer back. "Hold it."

He stared at the slumped figure, expecting to see the man make a quick move for a gun. The only thing that moved was his head, which dropped a little lower to the floor. Then the man's hand slipped off the door latch and hit the small board platform fronting the door with a hollow thud.

"Shit." The man laughed, but when he spoke his voice was thin and pinched, as though he were on the verge of tears. "They wouldn't fucking let me in!"

Longarm slid his eyes around, looking for anyone who might be slipping around him. Staring down his Winchester's barrel at the silhouette piled up in front of the door, he kept his voice hard, even, and low. "Throw out your weapons, Todd."

California Todd chuckled bizarrely. "I ain't got no weapons."

"Who's in the cabin?"

"Woolyard." Todd's voice pinched again into a kind of sob. "And that fuckin' bitch of a daughter of his." He rammed the door with the back of his hand and sobbed for real this time. "They wouldn't let me in when the cows came, and I'm all busted up!"

Longarm looked at the dark window left of the front door.

It was a velvet square without reflection, which meant it probably had no glass. He couldn't see or hear anyone inside.

"Woolyard!" he called. "Throw out your weapons and hobble on out here. Your men are dead and your cattle are scattered to hell and gone. Probably be in Wichita by mornin'. Your daughter, too. Both of you get your asses out here *now*!"

In the window, a gun flashed and barked. The slug tore over Longarm's left shoulder and pinged into the ground just behind him. Though momentarily blinded by the gun's flash, he aimed at the window and fired two quick rounds. Both hammered an inside wall.

"*No!*" Verna Woolyard yelped.

Longarm racked a fresh shell and gritted his teeth with fury. He opened his mouth to shout another order but stopped when a dog barked somewhere off the cabin's left side. He jerked his head in that direction. A figure was slumped low at the cabin's front corner, the starlight touching a rifle barrel.

Longarm aimed and fired three furious shots. Amid the Winchester's blasts, he heard the smacks of two bullets tearing through flesh. A man screamed, and there was the crunch of a body falling in gravel, and the metallic clatter of a rifle doing likewise.

The dog—it had to be Louie; Longarm would have recognized that high, brittle bark anywhere—whimpered and skulked off into the brush.

"Papa!" Verna's scream echoed inside the cabin.

Running feet thudded the packed earth of the cabin's interior. The door clicked and squawked open. A slender, blond-headed figure bolted out of the cabin, tripped over California Todd still sitting just outside the door, and hit the ground with a moan.

Longarm kept his rifle aimed at the girl, but as she climbed to her feet, sobbing shrilly, he saw that she had no

gun. She ran over to the figure slumped just off the cabin's
left shoulder and dropped to her knees.

"Papa, don't die!" she half-shouted, half-wailed.

Woolyard grunted and groaned.

His daughter jerked her face toward Longarm, a pale oval
from which green eyes glittered in the darkness. "You killed
him, you bastard!"

Longarm glanced at California Todd, who now lay flat on
his back in front of the cabin, laughing hysterically, insanely.
The lawman kept his rifle aimed at the girl as he strolled over
and looked down at her father, who must have slipped out of
the cabin through a back door.

"Oh, you killed him!" she wailed, laying her head on her
father's chest.

Woolyard lay on his back, chest heaving. Blood shone
darkly up high on his right shoulder. More shone on his right
temple, but that wound appeared a graze.

"He'll live," Longarm grumbled, slipping the man's revolver from his holster and tossing it over toward one of his
men—the Mexican cook—who lay dusty and dead. He did
the same with Woolyard's rifle. "I'll do better next time."

"Oh, Daddy," Verna wailed, lifting her head to stare into
her father's pain-racked eyes. "Don't die and leave me.
Please don't! He'll . . . he'll—" She looked up at Longarm
again, and set her jaws angrily. "No telling what he'll do."

"Well, for starters," Longarm said, "I'll be haulin' your
sassy little ass off to the hoosegow for a good long time on
charges of murder, cattle rustling, international conspiracy,
fraud, and a few other things I'm sure the suits'll come up
with. But don't worry—dear old Daddy will be along to join
you. He might be stove up for a while, but he'll be there.
He'll hold your hand while they walk you both up the gallows steps."

Woolyard coughed and turned his head toward Longarm. "How . . . how in the hell did you know where to find us?"

"Tracked you. Started from where you left Hall and Tremaine hanging like a couple of dressed-out beeves."

"I had no hand in that," Woolyard grunted, running the heel of his hand across his bloody temple, then dropping his chin to get a look at his shoulder. "My men did that."

"Save it for the judge, you murderin' old bastard. What'd they do—send a rider for you after you'd killed Hall and Tremaine and I'd slipped away, to tell you the jig was up? That your green canyon along with your stolen cattle—cattle you stole from your own company—had been found? *Time to head to Mexico?*"

"Don't say anything, Papa," Verna said, planting her hands on both sides of her father's face and staring into his eyes. "We don't have to tell him anything. We'll get a good lawyer, and—"

"You'll still hang," Longarm said.

"Please," Woolyard begged Longarm. "Don't be too hard on her. This was my idea. She just went along with it because we had few other choices."

"Few other choices than to steal cattle from the company you work for?"

"That's right." Woolyard rested his gray, curly-haired head back in the dirt. He was still breathing hard. Verna had lain her head on his chest and was weeping uncontrollably. "The ranch wasn't making money. Losing money, in fact. The company was threatening to sell or just close it down. Rustlers, twisters, drought, falling cattle prices . . ."

"So you concocted this scheme—you and your men—to rustle your own beef, blame it on the settlers leasing state school land, like Miguel Corpus, and trail it down across the Rio Grande to sell in Mexico. You would have gotten a better price here in the U.S., but too many questions would have been asked, too many papers would have been required, concerning the Pleasant Valley brand."

Woolyard's face dropped, and he stretched his lips back from his teeth in pain and frustration. "Ah, shit. Why'd they have to send *you*, fer chrissakes?"

"I'll ask the questions, Woolyard. Who the hell shot you in the ass?"

"Rustlers," Woolyard grunted, wincing again. "Not my own men, of course. The range teems with the bloody bastards!"

"Why'd you put me, Hall, and Tremaine on that trail into the lava bluffs? You sent us straight toward your hidden herd."

Woolyard said nothing. He ran a hand through Verna's hair, lifting her head slightly. "Do me a favor, girl," he rasped. "Take off my bandana, shove it into my shoulder."

As Verna did what she'd been told, Longarm stared down at Woolyard, his brows drawn down in thought. "You bastard," he muttered finally, as the girl shoved the wadded bandana into the wound in her father's shoulder. "You sent us out there to kill us nice and quiet."

Longarm clenched a fist, remembering the two carcasses hanging from the oak tree. "You probably sent a rider out ahead of us or around us to alert the others. Out there, we'd disappear and never be seen or heard from again. Likely even a battalion of cavalry riders wouldn't find us. Our disappearance would be blamed on the other settlers. Probably on Corpus.

"Shit, the army and the other lawman who'd just naturally be sent out here to investigate would be so busy investigating the innocent ranchers that you and your men could have just slipped slick as shit off to Mexico with the herd. Probably stayed down there, out of the jurisdiction of the American authorities, for the rest of your lives."

Verna jerked another angry look at Longarm, her eyes flashing, her bosom heaving behind her brown wool cape. "What choice did we have? The company was going to sell. With a failure like that—due to no fault of my father's—his reputation would be ruined! We'd have nowhere to go!"

Longarm wanted to tell her she'd have made a good whore, but he held his tongue. Instead, he turned away and walked over to California Todd, who lay silently now on his back in front of the cabin.

Longarm knelt down. The man's eyes were open, but his chest wasn't moving. He was battered and bloody, cut up savagely by the hooves of the stampeding herd. Longarm removed a glove and held the back of his hand against the sheriff's nose.

No breath. The man was dead.

"Damn, Todd," Longarm said, remembering Hall and Tremaine's story of the man's hard life, which had included Todd's being shot by accident by his own commanding officer during the War, after he'd gone to so much trouble to stay out of action. "No matter how hard they try—some folks just can't get a break."

The thuds of running hooves sounded on his right. He stood, holding out his rifle. He lowered it when he saw the single rider leading three saddled horses, and heard Ana Corpus's voice pitched with caution.

"Custis? Is that you there?"

Her rifle barrel flashed in the starlight.

"Ana, I'm damn sure relieved you didn't get caught under them cows."

Ana leaped out of the saddle. "They were south of me, but I heard them. Thought there was an earthquake at first. What hap—?"

She gasped when she turned toward Woolyard and his

daughter, who was fashioning a sling with her father's belt for his arm. "Ayee!" she said, shocked. "What . . . ?"

"Long story."

"Who is that by the door?"

"That there is Sheriff California Todd. He done got caught in another stampede."

Ana looked up at Longarm. "Another one?"

"Yeah, he's been stampeded for years. Funny thing about such folks. Most of 'em get trampled because they tend to throw themselves under cows."

Later that night, after Woolyard and his daughter had been locked in the cabin, and Longarm and Ana had set up camp outside, near where the rustlers' cook fire had been, Longarm lay awake staring at the stars.

He was rolling the details of Woolyard's scheme through his mind again, finding himself shaking his head as it all came clear. Apparently the ranch manager had been using his own men as well as seasoned border bandits to gather and move his herd—rustling just a few at a time until he had as many as he figured he needed for a tidy grubstake for him and his daughter in Mexico.

Blaming the rustling on the state land settlers had been a smoke screen. All the better a screen because likely some of them had, indeed, been rustling Pleasant Valley beef, though on a far smaller scale than Woolyard's own men.

He'd no doubt put California Todd on his roll because he'd needed the sheriff on his side against Corpus and the other school land settlers. Also, he probably figured he'd needed a go-between, and who better than the local law to handle any outside lawmen—including stock detectives, Texas Rangers, and deputy U.S. marshals—who'd likely come snooping around the rustling grounds?

Longarm chuckled dryly at the Scotsman's audacity.

"Can't sleep?" Ana lifted her head from her saddle, which was wedged up close to Longarm's.

"Too damn much excitement, I reckon."

"Maybe I can help."

Ana lifted her arms, and there was a rustle of cloth as she lifted her camisole up and over her head, and tossed it away. Her breasts stood up proud on her chest, softly limned by blue starlight. Ana shook her hair back from her face, then leaned forward and wrapped her arms around Longarm's neck.

"I owe you a lot, Custis. With the war over, Pa-Pa won't have to sell his herd, and we can stay at Wolf Creek."

"Ah, hell," Longarm said.

He felt as though he'd been trampled by the stampeding herd, but his ever-ready trouser snake stirred. He cupped the girl's breasts in his hands, rolled her nipples under his thumbs, and kissed her.

A mewling sounded.

Ana gasped and jerked back, turning her head in the direction of the odd, feral sound.

Longarm turned that way, as well. California Todd's coyote-dog had stolen into the camp earlier, a good-sized beef bone in its mouth. It had been working on the bone for the past hour or so, only a few feet away, growling low and groaning in pleasure as it gnawed the Woolyard crew's supper.

"Don't mind him," Longarm said. "That's my friend, Louie. He's right friendly once you get to know him."

He wrapped his arms around Ana's smooth, slender waist and, kissing her, moved her back against his saddle.

Watch for

**LONGARM AND THE ARIZONA ASSASSIN**

the 373<sup>rd</sup> novel in the exciting LONGARM
series from Jove

*Coming in December!*